SLOANE

BOOK ONE OF SLOANE

NICHOLAS KURCH

SLOANE
NICHOLAS KURCH

 Love Knot Books

https://loveknotbooks.ca

Love Knot Books is an imprint of DAOwen Publications

Copyright © Nicholas Kurch

All rights reserved

Sloane / Nicholas Kurch

Edited by MJ Moores and Douglas Owen

Cover art by MMT Productions and Infinite Pathways

ISBN 978-1-928094-57-9
EISBN 978-1-928094-58-6

10 9 8 7 6 5 4 3 2 1

To Olivia

1

SLOANE

The once warm, idyllic air turned chill and robbed the earth of its vibrance as the yellow taxi arrived at the Hotel Imperial. The hotel resided on the edge of the scenic resort town of Riders Bay, a town which had lost its luster years ago. The overcast sky accentuated the scent of dew permeating the thinning air. Soon, it seemed, the air would thin until there was nothing left to breathe.

"There's supposed to be clear skies all weekend long," the driver said, turning around to face his female passenger as the taxi screeched to a halt. "Hell, it looks to me like a storm's brewing."

The woman peered at the greyed sky, pondering all she would soon wrought. She slyly grinned paying the fare. "I shouldn't be here longer than the weekend," she said in her posh British accent.

She scanned the exterior of the hotel standing aside the taxi while the driver took her bags from the trunk. The nearby, overgrown shrubbery browned from inattentiveness just as the paint on the hotel faded, and the walkway cracked. A raise of her eyebrows betrayed an awareness of the lack of care the old building received. The hotel would not be fit for her, but thought it would have to do as she moved into the lobby.

The woman brushed aside her long, wavy, blonde hair letting it cascade down the middle of her back as she strode up to the concierge desk. Her stilettos clacked on the scuffed black and white tile floor of the hotel lobby, echoing in the empty space. She slowly consumed the bellhop with her eyes, absorbed as he was with his smartphone, before he sprung up to help with her bags.

The concierge, transfixed by her rather large novel, didn't realize she had company. The woman read the girl's name tag: Mary.

The blonde cleared her throat. Mary put down her steamy romance with the tattered cover, yellowing pages, and a "used" tag from the local library. She straightened up and put on a bright smile. The woman knew she would be one of only a few guests during the offseason and this worked to her advantage.

"Can I help you, ma'am?" the girl asked politely.

"I hate being called *ma'am*. The name's Sloane."

"Okay, Miss Sloane–"

"No, no, my dear." Sloane waved off the receptionist's words as she fluttered her lush eyelashes. "We're friends now. Please Mary, it's Sloane. Just Sloane."

"Okay, Sloane. How can I–"

"You see I'm quite late, aren't I?"

"Yes. Check-in was two hours past."

"No, no. I mean to say, I should have arrived at a sooner date as to confirm."

"Um, confirm what, Miss– I mean, Sloane?"

"Should I tell you?" Sloane bit her lip nervously. "Well,

seeing as how we are basically old friends now, Mary,"—Sloane rested her hand softly onto the girl's as she whispered —"I'll tell you. But I must warn you, it is a great deal of gossip. Okay?"

Mary nodded, uncertain.

"It all began when my ex-boyfriend's sister's ex-husband's other stepson from a previous marriage was in trouble. You see, I was very fond of the lad as he was growing up. Then he was accepted to attend university. He was the very first in his family, and it was the only opportunity to leave the small backward coal-mining town. The whole town hadn't even accepted the concept of singing or dancing. Quite backward."

Sloane pursed her lips as Mary leaned in. "Really?" she asked, intrigued.

Sloane leaned forward as well. "Oh, yes. But the poor young man was not of money, and no one else would pay. So, I put it upon myself to give him the money for his studies. I wanted to be of as much assistance as I could. I wired him the money every month for a year, until eventually I received a very disturbing call in the dead of night while out on safari, hunting ivory poachers."

"What was the call about?" Mary asked, breathlessly.

"I'll tell you. The young man had been mugged. All of his money and all the school books needed were stolen. He was severely beaten in the attack. He would have died had it not been for a monastery of Buddhists who took it upon themselves to heal him. I flew eight thousand and a half miles to be with him and help him recover. I asked why the monks hadn't helped him during the assault, and they said it was because they were strictly non-violent."

"What the hell do they think about people getting beat up right in front of them?" Mary said exacerbated. "I can't believe it. Then what happened?"

Sloane did all she could to suppress a slight smile. How effortless it had been to bring this quaint young woman into her grasp. Now, though, the time came to reel her in with the emotional gut punch. She eyed the paperback resting under Mary's clasped hands.

"Together, he and I stayed at the monastery as he recovered. While there, I learned two very important things about myself. One, I found religion and the ancient teachings of Karma. I learned the importance of paying kind acts forward."

Mary nodded. "I completely agree with that. I so believe in helping those in need."

"I know."

"And the second thing?" she asked.

"That I was desperately in love with that young man. He was fifteen years my junior, but we didn't care. Age was nothing to us but a number. We furiously made love at the monastery over the next six months."

Mary clutched her heavy novel, tearing small pieces off the pages. Her teeth chattered anxiously, and her eyes grew wide. Sloane took the girl's fingers into both of her hands to save the book.

"That is, until he left. Nigel, that's his name, was so vibrant, if you know what I mean. So strong. I realized I wasn't helping him, he was helping me."

"Where did he go? Why did he leave?" Mary's eyes glistened with unshed tears.

"He's here. In Riders Bay. It turns out he lied to me and the monks about why he was attacked. He wasn't being mugged, you see. He owed the mob for a gambling debt."

"He lost all of your money gambling?" Mary's eyes widened.

"Poker, to be precise."

"How could he betray you like that?"

"You see, it isn't what you think."

"What was it?"

"He was gambling to pay for his best friend's roommates'

mother's cancer treatment. They didn't have the money, so they thought they could gamble for it. Illegally, of course. The mob is after him for the rest of it now."

"Oh, my God. But he's the love of your life."

"I know. I'd do anything for my dearest, Nelson."

"I thought you said his name was Nigel?"

Shit.

"It is. Nigel Nelson."

"Then what?" Mary asked, shaking off her last comment.

"I told the mob boss, Big Columbo, I'd pay the money in a month. That was three months ago."

"How much money?"

"Five hundred thousand dollars."

"Oh, my God."

"I know." Sloane cast her eyes at their still-clutched hands. "I'm – excuse my French – totally fucked."

"I'd say."

Sloane looked up, straight into Mary's eyes. "And that's the other reason I'm here. To get the money."

"From where? From who? From Nigel Nelson?"

"No, from Nathan."

"Who's Nathan?" Mary's grip tightened on Sloane's hand.

"Nathan Nelson. Nigel Nelson's illegitimate brother from their mother's second marital affair with Nolan Nelson."

"Nigel took the name of his mother's side-piece?"

"No. They were both named Nelson. They were all cousins."

"Oh, my God."

"I know. So tragic."

"So, Nathan has the money?"

"Yes."

"And he's in town with Nigel?'

"No, Nathan inherited the money from Nolan, and Nathan wants to pay Nigel with Nolan's money."

"I see. I think. This all seems really fantastic. I don't know about any of this." Mary's grip loosened and she pulled her hands away. Sloane gripped the girl's fingers just tight enough to convince her not to walk away.

"I understand your hesitance to believe a formerly complete stranger, but I am indeed in danger. I so desperately need your help, Mary."

"What do you mean?"

"All this time we've been talking, I feel we've become sisters."

"I get that. I'm told I'm very approachable." She leaned back toward Sloane.

"I need you, my sweet."

"Aw. I'm your sweet?"

"That's what I called my late sister, when she was still alive."

"What happened to her?"

"She was killed by her ex-husband."

"Oh, my God. Nigel killed her?"

"No. Nathaniel did it. Nigel Nelson's best friend from grammar school."

"Another Nelson."

"You do catch on."

"How can I help?"

"I need a place to stay. Somewhere off the books. If the mob knows I'm here, they will kill me."

"Say no more. I'll leave work right away. You can stay at my house until we figure this out."

Sloane's eyes darted back and forth at the unexpected detour in her plan. Before she could lose control of the situation, she gripped Mary's hands tighter.

"No, we can't. I knew you'd say that because you're very maternal. I could tell just by looking at you. I have to protect you, which means we can never be seen near each other. In fact, we can never even speak to one another again. It's for your own protection. I *have* to protect you. I won't fail you the way I failed my mother who died in a terrible potato extraction accident."

"Oh, my God."

"Yes."

"I know. You can stay here."

"Could I?"

"Yes, of course."

"I haven't any money. Not right now, anyway."

"Say no more." Mary typed on the computer. "I can put you in–"

"The Presidential Suite, if it's available. I want to have a lot of space to hide just in case the mob come looking. You know, room to room."

"Oh my–"

"I know." Sloane looked down and bit her bottom lip.

"Yes, of course. The Presidential Suite." Mary looked over to the bellhop. "Robbie, take Sloane's bags to the top suite, and keep it quiet."

"Yeah, okay," Robbie said nervously, having heard the entire conversation.

Sloane nodded in appreciation. "Thank you. Again, remember, we may never see or even speak to each other again. I must keep you safe."

The blonde held up Mary's hand to her cheek. They both teared up as they said their final goodbyes.

"I'll always keep you safe, my sweet," Mary said.

"Thank you. I'll always remember you."

Sloane walked away one tentative step at a time, extending her arm until she and Mary had to let go. She moved a few steps to the elevator Robbie held when she turned back and returned to Mary.

"Yes, my sweet?" Mary asked eagerly.

"The room key."

2
_____

ANDY

Andrew Simmons was a simple yet sarcastic man of limited taste and far less experience. He sat in his accounting firm office, in the coastal town of Riders Bay, brushing his hands through his simple haircut, messing it up and fixing it – only to mess it up again. A windowless box with a door acted as his office. He scowled at the light-blue paint as it chipped away from the wall as much as it chipped at his soul.

"Andy," the muffled voice said from just outside his office.

He'd been sitting on his cheap, uncomfortable chair since the morning. He wiggled his toes in his sensible black leather shoes to regain some feeling, which he lost on a daily basis, anywhere if not just his feet.

Andy didn't look up. "Yes, Jerry. Come in."

He'd known it would be Jerry before Jerry even knocked.

"Hey, Andy." Jerry waddled into the office, his shoes

squeaking as he walked, a large lop-sided grin on his face. If a dog ever evolved into a human being, he'd be Jerry.

The sort of person who never made any friends, ever, Jerry would end up dying alone. Andy worked with him and, naturally, a friendship evolved, but only because neither of them would have anyone else to talk with otherwise.

"You going to the gala tonight?" he asked wiping sweat from his pale bald head. "Should be a lot of fun."

Andy almost burst out laughing.

The Riders Bay Annual Gala existed only for those of wealth and influence, while the rest of town stayed away, either by disinterest or by threat of unemployment. The town Andy had called home since birth was no longer what it used to be. Riders Bay had seen better days.

It was springtime, offseason for the working residents of the town. Most of the commerce revolved around seasonal vacationers. The piers which brought in crab and lobster sat empty this time of year, and therefore, the variety of food became drastically limited to whatever trucked in on a weekly basis. When it shut down during the offseason, Riders Bay became a ghost town.

The last few years, following a tough recession, made it nearly impossible for the working-class to remain working. It became a hard truth to swallow for many of the proud townsfolk, but they swallowed it regardless.

When tourists didn't want to spend their vacations in Riders Bay, the hotels didn't require the services of their restauranteurs. When the restaurants slowed down their business, services of the fishermen were no longer necessary. Thus, the piers shut down because they were only equipped to operate six months out of the year, and it could no longer be deemed viable to stay open much longer if business continued failing.

No hotel business meant there would be no need for hotel staff. Staff stopped regularly taking their earnings to buy things at local stores and the use of services from local mechanics, electricians, plumbers, carpenters, and all assortments of laborers and crafts-workers in Riders Bay slowed.

When business struggled for some, it struggled for all – even for accountants like Andy and Jerry.

Andy turned to face Jerry. "You know I don't want to go to that stupid gala. So, I'm not going."

"There'll be a lot of clients there. And a lot of potential ones as well. This sort of cajoling could really help this firm boost to the next level. So, what do ya say? Could I get you to come by?"

"Not interested." Andy looked down at his computer pretending to work.

"Oh, you should probably change before we go." Jerry gestured to Andy's clothes.

Andy looked down at himself. His khaki pants and checkered shirt were stained yellow. He'd eaten in his office; a sandwich he'd put too much mustard on. Most of it got on his clothes instead of in his mouth.

"Aw, shit," Andy exclaimed as he wiped at the stains.

Jerry laughed. "Your lunch is supposed to go in you, not on you."

"I'm still not going to that stupid thing tonight. So, no, I don't have to change."

"Come on, buddy, show some company spirit."

"Why?"

"What do you mean, why?"

"I mean, why me?"

"Well, because you're a junior partner, that's why."

"I really mean, why is this my life?" Andy leaned back and his cheap, noisy office chair creaked. "I've been working here for almost fifteen years. I started doing this just after I graduated from college. I have nothing else, and that's because I barely sought out anything else."

"Well, maybe that's kinda, sorta, totally your fault." Jerry braced himself. He had good reason to. Andy's eyes widened with rage as his hand hovered over his stapler, compelled to throw it at Jerry's sweaty ham-shaped head.

"Either way," Andy continued, attempting to calm himself by talking. "This is my life every day, and if for once I don't want to go to a thing, I shouldn't have to."

"Oh, okay," Jerry said sarcastically as he chuckled.

Andy didn't pay attention as he found more mustard on his tan jacket. "Damn it." He frantically wiped away the mustard from his clothes with a bunch of napkins still on his disorderly desk.

"Why is it I can't come to my boring job, sit in my boring office, do my boring work, then go home to my quiet boring house? Why are you throwing a monkey-wrench in my best laid plans of self-imposed boredom? Why can't you leave me in peace?"

Jerry chuckled as he left Andy's office. "You're so funny. I'll see you there. Eight o'clock at the Country Club."

"I'm not going!" Andy yelled after him.

Alongside being a hanger-on and other things, Jerry just so happened to be Andy's superior.

So, Andy would be going to the stupid gala.

3

ANDY

The low hum of house music played over the speakers in the timber-laced dining hall of the Country Club. The hum acted as melatonin for the soul and could drive the hyperactive to coma. Andy sat at the bar, struggling against the sensation to close his heavy eyelids as the gala wore on through the night.

The low-wattage yellow fluorescent lights weren't making his attempts to remain conscious any easier. He scanned the attendees of the gala, checking each face, one after another, for those who may seem like-minded. As Andy observed, he saw what were once wrinkled faces straining to show any emotion other than shock, grappling against their Botox and multiple facelifts. These were the rich and aimless. The ones with wealth who could trace their ancestry to the men on the money.

Andy did, finally, find those in the hall who seemed most likely to want to set fire to themselves than have to listen to another cackle over a lame joke. He noticed their faces sink further into despair with each tug representing another attendee wanting another drink or another hors d'oeuvre. Those were the staff. The only ones in the building for whom Andy did taxes. The only people he wanted to converse with but couldn't for fear he'd get one of them fired on the spot. Fired by so-called people who didn't care to see things from any other perspective than their own.

So, instead of pointlessly attempting to engage with anyone, Andy drowned his boredom at the bar. Next to him stood Jerry, bobbing his head off-beat to the humming music that seemed to move from the overhead speakers to Andy's molars. Jerry's shit-eating grin gave him a migraine.

"This is a better turnout than last year's gala, I think," Jerry said.

Andy glowered. "They have one of these things every month. Just slap a different name on it and drink to excess, that's what they do. Don't they know this gala should be for everyone in town?"

"What do you mean?" Jerry asked, puzzled.

"Riders Bay is for all tourists, not just the rich ones."

"What other kind of tourists does Riders Bay get?"

"You know what I mean. Every winter and every summer people are supposed to come on vacation. When are any of us, the regular people, the ones who actually keep this town up, supposed to go on vacation?"

"Like you said, the fall and the spring, when our guests aren't here anymore. That's when we go on vacation. When else would we go?"

Andy side-eyed Jerry as he sipped his drink.

"It seems *they're* always on vacation," Andy said into his beverage referring to the wealthy attendees.

Jerry faced the dance floor where many of the elite milled about. Andy sat firmly with his back to everyone. The only person's attention he wanted going forward would be the bartender's.

"And the reason there's more people than last year's gala is because some of the people who showed up aren't even from here," Andy explained. "They're just here for the free food and open bar."

"Oh, this isn't an open bar," the bartender said.

"Well, shit. You could have told me that five vodka tonics ago, Mike."

"Sorry."

"These are all potential clients, Andy, and they're good people." Jerry patted Andy's back. "Let's start working to get their business."

"These people aren't good people. They couldn't care less about us or, for that matter, this town's struggles. When this place crumbles away and shuts down for good, they'll just take their vast wealths somewhere else," Andy said, slurring.

"Like where?"

"Just off the top of my head, there are the Islands of Montoon."

"Didn't they just have a civil war?"

"Okay, if not there, then what about Saint Francis?"

"I don't think I know anyone here who skis. And that place is kind of a party town."

"Yeah, everyone here is pretty stuffy."

Andy looked over his shoulder at the small gathering and sipped his drink. He knew these people; he'd known them for years. The imminent closure of the town many of them had come to for decades, and for whom others had called home since birth, would do little to shake them from their apathy.

"These people don't care. Just look at them."

"I think you're being too harsh." Jerry frowned. "They're all active members of the community."

Andy chuckled. "Really? You really think they care? Then where's the rest of the town?"

"I don't know, turning in early to sleep, maybe?"

"There are hundreds of people who live in Riders Bay, but as I look around I see a few dozen. And it ain't because everyone's going to sleep early tonight. There's about fifty people at this thing, and that includes the staff and the DJ they bused in from the city. Then there's the two of us."

"What does that mean?"

"We don't belong here, Jerry."

"I don't know about that."

"We're neither rich, nor do we work here."

Andy pointed over to the side of the room at a tall, striking man. "Take Jack Buck over there. That handsome, arrogant, dimwit hasn't had a hot blockbuster in twenty years, but he's here. Why? Because he's famous and everyone seen near him seems just as famous. Yet, he rests on his laurels, shining in the dimming glow of this own stardom. And the movie he thinks he's famous for was a piece of shit."

"I liked it."

"Then there's those two pretentious, pedantic... I ran out of words that apply to them that start with the letter P, but you get what I mean."

Andy pointed to the other side of the room at a very sharply dressed couple.

"You mean Abagail and Walter Jonas?" Jerry asked.

"Yeah."

"I think they're all right. I handle their taxes and other financial affairs."

"You mean Abagail's massive inheritance from her dead dad's estate? That's the only thing that's sustaining their lofty lifestyle."

"Doesn't she play the flute or something?" Jerry asked scrunching up his nose in thought.

"The violin, I think. But she ain't making money playing it. And Walter, I mean, Jesus. The guy won't shut the hell up about the Eighth Century. The goddamned Eighth Century. Not all of history, just the Eighth Century."

"I get it, Andy, Walter likes the Eighth Century."

"The guy talked my ear off for like an hour about that shit. No one cares about the fucking Eighth Century."

"Well, he does."

"Look at them. They're literally sticking their noses up at everyone."

"You really think that's what they're doing? I just thought they had overly great posture."

"They're ridiculous."

"Or maybe they have neck problems or something."

"Then we have the biggest gaping assholes at this whole thing." Andy fully turned around on his barstool as he gestured at a family of three in the very middle of the dance floor. "The Rosenbaum's," he said with noticeable distain.

"Why do you have to refer to them as gaping assholes?"

"Because they are. They think they run this town. Why? Because they have the most money?"

"Yeah, that's probably why."

"Because they're the most influential?"

"Oh, yeah that too."

"Whatever. Of everyone here, the ones I've mentioned are by far what's so wrong with this so-called community. And that's who they think good people are. People like them."

"Maybe you should slow down on the tonics, eh, Andy."

"And you want their business."

Andy turned back around on his barstool, putting his back to the rest of the attendees once again.

"If they wanted to give us business we would have gotten it twenty years ago. They don't need us. Hell, I'm not even sure they like us."

"Well, where else are they all going to get their massive amounts of taxes done?" Jerry asked sincerely.

"These people don't pay massive amounts of taxes. They

write everything off. That's why they have a party every month and call it a charitable event. Secondly, they get their taxes done by big shots in the city, which we are not."

"Yeah, not with that attitude."

"What's it going to take?"

"What do you mean?"

"For you to leave me alone?" Andy mumbled into his drink.

"Huh?"

"Nothing."

"And what do we have here?" a loud, grumpy voice said from directly behind him. Andy glanced over his shoulder as Jerry did all the talking.

"Well, hello there, Mister Rosenbaum. How are you this evening?"

"I see Alliance Accounting sent their finest," Rosenbaum said.

Andy didn't want to listen to their annoying conversation. He wanted to walk off, or at the very least for Rosenbaum to walk off… a cliff.

"Yes, sir. And actually, it's Allied Accounting."

"Did I ask to be corrected?"

"Well, no, of course not, sir. No one really asks to be corrected."

"Except when they say, 'correct me if I'm wrong,' which I never said."

"That's very bold, sir, very bold."

"Of course. And that's why I'm a titan of industry."

"Which industry?"

"All of them, son. All of them. Who do you think lobbied legislatures to start investing with the teachers' pension plans?"

"Uh–"

"That's right. Me."

"Is that really something you want to go around bragging

about?" Andy asked, again mumbling into his drink, which he sipped slower now that he knew he had to pay for it.

"Exactly, son." Rosenbaum slapped Andy's back. "And good things came from it as well."

Andy shivered in revulsion at Rosenbaum's touch. The man acted as an insult to everything Riders Bay used to stand for. Andy counted the seconds until he could leave.

"The recession screwed the market, and the teachers lost their pensions. Let's give you a parade," Andy mumbled.

"Nope, never got thanked for it either," Rosenbaum said with a hint of pride. "Thankless job being an investment banker. We're just the ones keeping civilization together, that's all. Why thank us?"

"I got a thank you for you, you son-of-a–"

"Take what's happening to this town for instance. Damned shame. Bad business-sense, that's all."

"Well, what would you suggest?" Jerry asked.

"Gentrification, of course."

Andy nearly spat out his drink.

"That's a fine idea, sir. The shot in the arm this town needs. Don't you think, Andy?" Jerry asked.

"Yeah, a gun shot."

"Where's your father anyway, Simons?" Rosenbaum hovered closer, his scotch-breath tickling the back of Andy's neck.

"Oh, Mister Simmons is out of town. He should be back tomorrow," Jerry replied for Andy with a dopey disposition, barely aware of Andy's ongoing impatience.

"Frank's a good man. A real straight shooter," Rosenbaum said.

"I completely agree," Jerry echoed.

"A little timid sometimes."

"I completely agree."

"But strong."

"I completely agree."

"Could use more backbone in business matters."

"I completely agree."

"But, otherwise, an all-around okay, regular sort of guy."

"I completely agree."

"Jerry," Andy said.

"Yes, Andy?"

"Stop agreeing."

"Yes, Andy."

"This town needs a change," Rosenbaum said. "Don't you think?"

"Oh, yes, sir. Of course. A little bit of change can't be all bad," Jerry said.

"And what about you, son?" he asked.

Jerry nudged Andy when he realized he hadn't heard Rosenbaum the first time.

Andy wheeled, nearly spilling the contents of his glass. He faced Rosenbaum's stern glare and immediately regretted it. Andy considered pivoting to ignore the red, puffy, glaring melon of a head.

"Excuse me. What was that?" Andy asked.

"I asked"– Rosenbaum grew impatient with each, huffing breath he took– "don't you think this town needs a change?"

"Sure."

"There you have it."

"Just not the one you're looking for."

"Excuse me?"

"You have a dark, dare I say, even limited perspective on the issues facing this town. The change you say you want isn't the change you'd like very much."

"Meaning?"

"Suppose you invested your considerable wealth in at least one of the local businesses. You'd begin to understand what's ailing this place. You'd be a part of this town, instead of just living here."

"I'll have you know I do invest in this town. Hell, just the other day I bought the services of two more maids. Tell me how that isn't investment?"

"Susan and Debra?"

"I think those are their names."

"Yeah, they used to own a bakery in town. It was open for years. Now they're maids for you."

"You're welcome."

"Never mind."

"What would you have me do, Simons?"

"Damn it, man. It's Simmons. You know that. We've known each other for over twenty-five years. I've had just about enough of your bullshit corporate mind tricks, pretending not to know someone's name to show they're not as important as you."

"I genuinely forgot your last name. Hell, I don't even really know this fellow's name." Rosenbaum pointed at a smiling Jerry with his thumb. "It's Gerald, right?"

"Close enough," Jerry and Andy said at the same time.

"And here's another tip." Andy burped slightly and began again. "If you want people to care about this community, or if you want to prove you actually care about Riders Bay, open this gala up to everyone, not just the rich people."

"We can't have common riffraff coming in here," Rosenbaum said.

"They're not riffraff. They're business owners and lifelong residents."

"It's not the same. Besides, how exclusive can this gala be? We invited you two."

"We can't thank you enough for that. Now, can we ask you for your business?" Jerry jumped in before Andy could tear Rosenbaum's head off.

"No. Of course not. I've been with the same accounting firm for over forty years. I'm not changing that now for some small-town hacks," he said, pointblank.

"You know what? I've had just about enough of you walking all over me and Gerald," Andy pointed.

"Thanks, Andy," Jerry said, appreciatively.

Andy stood up from his bar stool, holding his half-filled glass of mostly melted ice. He wobbled toward Rosenbaum and pointed at the stern man, ready to launch his tirade against the business-bully, when the doors to the dining hall crashed open.

Everyone craned their heads toward the main doors as the air suddenly cooled.

The space filled with a hushed quiet. Not a single person moved or spoke. After a moment, the loud clacking of stilettos echoed across the old, wooden floor.

Andy, in the midst of preparing himself for his tirade, halted. All eyes in the dining hall, including his own, transfixed on the woman who announced her arrival without so much as a single word.

All other thoughts escaped Andy. His entire focus remained on the glowing, tall, well-dressed woman. He made it his business to know who was and who wasn't a regular resident. It was clear this gorgeous woman had never been to Riders Bay before. In fact, he was sure he'd never seen a woman quite like her in his entire life.

She threw off her fur coat, drenched from the rain, and moved through the hall. Every step made a thunderous crack in the silent space.

The woman luminesced as she passed under the faulty fluorescent lights. Her earrings and necklace glistened in the soft shine. The glow of her jewelry placed her face in a constant soft-focus, and Andy looked upon her as though she were a dream. Her make-up looked professionally done. She flounced her way through the room in noticeably expensive red-bottom heels, her red dress dancing across the floor. What Andy couldn't understand about the enigmatic woman was who she tried to impress.

Her slender, fit frame glided through the space as bright emerald eyes glimmered past luscious, long eyelashes. Smoky eyeshadow conveyed a sense of mystery though her overall expression was slightly smug, as if she knew something about everyone that no one else did.

She stuck her nose up at every person she passed, incurious with whom any of them might be. This only made Andy adore her more. As she stalked past the attendees of the gala, they all averted their gazes.

They parted from her path as she swept past them.

Andy was fortunate no one looked his way, otherwise they would have seen the big, wide smile he wore as he gazed at this magnificent and mysterious woman. A woman who, by all appearances, knew exactly where she was going and what she was doing.

And who, by all appearances, headed straight for the bar and Andy.

4

SLOANE

"It'll do," Sloane said, scoffing at the Presidential Suite.

The two-thousand-square-foot space had three bedrooms, a breakfast nook, two and a half bathrooms, two dining areas, and three walk-in closets – one of which seemed to be entirely for shoes. The truly impressive suite was meant for royalty.

Sloane didn't care about the space, though it appeared to be the only immaculate thing in the entire town. She didn't care about the town. No, she only cared about the people in the town, and what they had to offer.

She considered it a total waste of her immensely precious and considerably valuable time being cooped up in her Presidential Suite. So, after only taking a half an hour in the room shoving her bags into the biggest closet she could find, she got right to work. She knew just where to start her inquiry on town affairs.

Sloane reapplied her bright red lipstick, checking herself in the mirror beside the entrance, before opening the door to her suite. She stuck out her long silky leg into the hall and peeked her head out. Robbie, the bellhop, stood at the end of the hall, his face aglow with the beam of his smartphone. She leaned her slender body, tight and flawless, against the door frame. Surely as the most interesting person who ever graced the grubby floors of the Hotel Imperial, Sloane knew Robbie would be there waiting. Either waiting to steal a glimpse of her as she left, or to simply find out what she was up to and report what he'd witnessed to the rest of the small-town folk.

"Bellboy," Sloane called out.

"Uh, yeah?" Robbie replied anxiously, standing up straight and shoving his phone in his pocket.

"Come over here." Sloane motioned Robbie to the door with her index finger, the light from her suite hit her from behind shrouding her face in darkness. She knew she cut an ominous figure in the doorway.

Robbie slowly approached. Sloane watched him gulping as the skinny young man meandered toward her with his hands in his pockets. He still wore his burgundy bellhop uniform and cap that were all a half-size too small for him

"Do they really make you wear that little outfit?" Sloane teased. "You look so adorable."

"Uh, thanks," Robbie gulped in reply.

"You are adorable. No… you're cute."

"I don't know about that."

"Oh, I'm sure of it. You must be beating them off with a stick."

"What do you mean?"

"The several lovers a week you must have."

"Nah."

"Yeah."

Sloane leaned forward as she giggled. She touched his arm and let her hand linger.

"What's the latest one's name?"

"Nah, I had to let that one go. I'm always looking forward to the next best thing."

"I'm sure you are."

Robbie's shoulders relaxed and he grinned. It didn't matter if what he said was even remotely true about his love life; all Sloane focused on was that he gave her what she wanted.

"So, if a handsome, completely untethered man like yourself were to take a lonely, out of town stranger out for a good time, what would you do?"

"I'd take you out."

She slapped him playfully on the arm.

"Who's to say I'm the one you're taking anywhere? This is completely hypothetical."

"Right, I'm sorry." Robbie's head and shoulders fell in awkward shame.

"It's perfectly fine, my dear." Sloane needed to salvage the moment. "You're not completely out of the question. I'm just wondering what a girl has to do to have some fun in this small town."

Robbie's head remained down as he stared at his dirty Chuck Taylors. Sloane gingerly lifted his chin with a single manicured finger, reverting his gaze onto her's. Her stare pierced his eyes.

"There—There's this swanky party at the Country Club," Robbie finally spat out.

"Country Club… swanky party you say?" Sloane clapped gleefully. "How wonderful. Call me a taxi."

Sloane pushed Robbie back and closed the door in his face. She needed to find something to wear for her coming out party.

A FEW HOURS LATER, she'd refreshed herself and changing into her evening gown. Sloane finally arrived downstairs to take her ride to the Country Club.

"It really is unseasonably cloudy," the driver said when they arrived.

Sloane saw the incredulous look the driver gave her through the rearview mirror. She knew he wasn't sure about her or her intentions.

"I'm sure no one will mind very much. I'll just pop in and get a lay of the land. Now you carry on, darling. I don't want to keep the only taxi in town from his fares any longer."

The gala had been going for hours when Sloane kicked her feet out of the back of the car to a waiting – closed door? Unsure why no one was there to announce her arrival, she simply went through the double-doors of the dining hall.

She watched everyone make an about-face toward the double-doors as she walked in. It took all she had not to mock their stunned silence. She had that effect on people.

At this point, she expected it.

As she glanced over at the other attendees, they looked away, almost afraid she'd rush over and bite their heads off for daring to even turn her way.

Everyone averted their gaze, all, except for the tall, poorly-dressed man standing at the bar with a ridiculous smile on his face.

Fascinated by this anomaly, Sloane strode over to the strange-looking man. The other two far less attractive men standing with him ducked their heads and moved away as she arrived at the bar.

"Vodka martini," Sloane said to the bartender. "And another of whatever my friend here is having. His drink has gotten rather watered down."

"Vodka tonic," the man replied.

"Very good," she said.

"So, we're friends already? That was fast."

"I'm a very friendly person." She grinned deviously, shifting closer to him to allow her lavender scented perfume to intoxicate him.

"I can see that." He breathed her in, half-closing his eyes. "You're the best person to be with at this thing."

"If you hate it so much, why are you still here?"

"Work stuff," he said leaning against the bar, trying to catch her eye.

"Work stuff. So boring." Sloane did not look at him. Instead, she focused on the bartender's mixing to ensure he got her drink right.

"Right? God, I hate it here."

"So, do I."

"You're pretty quick to judge. You new in town?"

"Oh, yes. Just came in."

"Sorry about the weather. Looks like a storm's coming or something."

"I'll just be passing through."

The man's quick wit gave him an odd charm. She would have some fun with him, but only if she promised herself to focus on what she came to Riders Bay for, first.

"So, what's a small town like this doing around a girl like you?" the man asked coolly.

"I'm looking for something fascinating. And I can tell you, so far, there's nothing fascinating here."

"Until you arrived."

"You're sweet. As sweet as they usually come."

"Want to get out of here?"

"That's forward of you. That's usually my thing."

"I mean for a walk. Trust me, I'm not that guy. I'm not going to try to sleep with you."

"That's too bad." Sloane's sultry tone wrapped around him as she finally turned and locked her gaze with his. "We just met."

Sloane looked around, and without another word, took

the man by the hand and hurried him out the side door overlooking the beach. She'd gotten what she'd come for. As expected, it hadn't taken long.

5

SLOANE

Sloane led him by the hand as they jogged away from the stuffy gala. They made it to a small paved road before she stopped. He tugged on her arm as he gestured with his head the direction they should go. She followed, gripping his hand tighter; a show of trust. She didn't actually know where she was going after all.

Her reflex to do something about how vulnerable she felt kicked in. Sloane wanted to regain control, but knew she had to bide her time. She didn't know the man who now guided her and fought the sensation to stiffen. The need to remain relaxed superseded all. She'd been in far more compromising situations. The key was to wait her turn to take control, to see what type of man he was as he guided them away from the gala.

He stopped when they reached the sand, and took off his shoes. Sloane felt naked as they released hands. The sensation of his palm on her's made her want to reach out for him.

Instead, she caressed it with her other hand. She stopped when he looked at her. His intense stare mesmerized her.

The man bewildered Sloane. She tried to shake the spell he'd somehow placed on her. Getting a handle on him would take a few beats, but she'd figure out what kind of man he was eventually. Something swelled within her, the onset of a sensation an adversary hadn't ever come close to making her feel before.

He gestured down with his head again, waiting for her to remove her heels before they continued. After a moment, he reached down, lifted one of her legs, and slipped off her stiletto. Finally, she snapped out of it, now enamored by the bold move as he did the same for the other foot. He handed her the heels before offering his hand again. She took the heels then his hand as he continued guiding her.

Clearly, the coastline of Riders Bay offered very little in terms of areas to lounge in the sun. A small sliver of what the locals termed "the beach" was scarce and neglected.

Even during an overcast night with hard winds, Sloane found the beach remarkable. Remarkable in that there weren't any hypodermic needles for them to step on as they walked bare foot on the sand.

"Tell me about yourself," she said.

He squeezed her fingers with his own, and coolly glanced sideways at her. Her heartbeat quickened, and she allowed herself a genuine smile. She didn't know what it meant; both her smile and his look, but was extremely intrigued.

The man was strange and unassuming, and she had to get to know him. He was absolutely disarming, but not because he was incredibly attractive; he was average. Nor because he was charming; he was only drunk. He was, instead, a riddle she needed to solve.

"Where do I start?" he replied.

"How about your name?"

"Of course. I'm Andy. Andy Simmons."

"Short for Andrew, I assume."

"Correct."

They walked over a small sand dune. Sloane almost didn't mind her feet getting sandy. It wouldn't be her job to clean them later, anyway.

"And what do you do for a living, Andrew?" Sloane asked.

"I'm an accountant," he said, almost reluctantly.

"Oh, really? How fascinating." She hid a yawn.

"Not really. It isn't fascinating in the slightest. It's the opposite, actually."

"What do you mean? All those numbers you have to count must make up for it."

"They're not just numbers."

"You're so right. It's money you're counting."

"Yeah. Anyway, I hate it."

"Why do you do it then?"

"It's my dad's firm. And his father did it before him, and so on to the beginning of time when all they had to account for were the amount of rocks someone had in the cave."

"Well, if you could do something else with your life, what would you do?"

Sloane watched the gears turn in his mind as he narrowed his eyes and cocked his head to one side. She knew this was a question he'd never gotten before. A question he'd never even asked himself.

He looked up in contemplation, then smiled. An idea formed as his eyes lit up, but then the look changed. His smile disappeared as he stared at the sand, frowning. It was as though he finally found out what he wanted in life and quickly realized it was something he could never have.

"I don't know," Andy said, a hitch in his voice. "I'd go on an adventure, maybe."

Sloane laughed.

"I know, it sounds corny." Andy pulled away from her a little. She tugged him back.

"It's not corny. It's cute. I think you're cute." Sloane playfully wrapped her arm around his to keep him close.

The dark waves pounded the shore; a roar so intense they had to wait between wave-crashes to speak. During the crashes they only looked at each other, eyes desperately searching to see beyond the surface. Sloane was disappointed when the waves finally settled down and they were forced to speak again.

"What do you do?" Andy asked.

"For money, you mean?" Sloane replied.

"Yeah."

"How best to put it? I'm a facilitator."

"What does that mean?"

"It means I facilitate the transfer of goods or money."

"Okay. So, where are you from? Wait, let me guess. England."

"What gave me away?"

"The haircut."

Sloane laughed and danced in front of Andy, walking backward holding both of his hands.

She didn't need him to say it. She wasn't even trying and she could tell that he would much rather be there on the smelly, gray beach than anywhere else in the world, especially the dull gala. Sloane was there for all of five minutes and even she wanted to set the place on fire to liven it up.

"And you're housesitting for someone?" Andy asked.

"Oh, no. I'm staying at the hotel. I have a beautiful suite." Sloane slipped back next to Andy's side as they walked.

"Nice. I only ask because most new people who come during the offseason are house-sitters. Or should I say mansion-sitters?"

"I didn't even know I could do that. Otherwise, that's what I'd be doing."

"Yeah, but you've got a great room. The hotel's nice, at least from what I recall of the last time I stayed there."

"When was that? A lot might have changed since then."

"My honey–" Andy cut himself off and stopped to look out at the ocean. He stood there, looking out into the abyss for so long, Sloane wondered if he'd become a statue. Then he sat down on the wet sand.

She rolled her eyes, gave a small shrug and sat down with him. "Do you want to talk–"

"So, how long have you facilitated?" Andy asked.

Sloane wasn't sure why Andy wanted to change the subject. Clearly, she'd struck a nerve, a nerve she wanted to keep striking.

"I don't know. It feels like my entire life. But what about you? Have you ever even left this–"

"So, what are you facilitating in Riders Bay?" Andy interrupted.

"Oh, it's nothing I'll bother you with, too much. Tell me about your father. Is he still with us?"

"No. He's just out of town."

She traced her hand up his arm, following the natural masculine contours. His glance caught her's as she traveled her hand higher up the inside. A smile flashed across her face as she shifted, hair cascading over her shoulder ever so slightly. He became slack jawed and his eyes dreamy. Grinning before coming to his senses for a moment.

"Are you working with someone in town?" Andy asked, slightly more sober. "Were you supposed to meet someone at the gala?"

She rolled her eyes. Ignoring the question, Sloane threw herself on top of Andy, straddling his waist, grabbing a handful of his hair on the back of his head, bringing his lips a breath away from her's. "I can't take any more of this flirting."

"What?" Andy asked in shock.

"Take me. No more foreplay. Take me right here, right now."

"On this dirty-ass beach?"

"I don't care who sees us. Do me."

"Do you?"

Sloane kissed Andy. She pulled him close, tugging on the lapels of his jacket. In that brief moment of laying it all bare, a thrill shocked up her spine as their tongues danced. His hands held her, and as their kiss deepened his grip on her grew tighter. Her chest pressed harder into his, feeling the warmth through their clothes. Her lungs burned as they gasped every time their lips weren't interlinked.

She had been with men she barely knew before, but not usually for very long. Certainly not with men she felt an immediate connection with. She wasn't sure where the electricity came from, but she certainly couldn't deny it in herself.

"Wait," Andy said, pulling away.

"No more waiting." With a single quick move, she undid his belt.

"I don't even know your name," Andy whispered into the nape of her neck as he breathed in the lilac of her shampoo.

"Names are so patriarchal."

Sloane let herself go; her heart rate climbing along with her temperature as Andy tried to resist her seduction and his meek attempts to be a gentleman.

Andy gripped her shoulders, the pitch in his voice rising. "No, they aren't. That doesn't even make any sense."

Sloane moved her hands up his chest, feeling his heart race. She finger-combed her hair back and moved in again to claim his mouth. Her lips locked with his, and after a moment his entire body enveloped her as his walls came down. He tried to maneuver away, but not enough to make her stop. She could tell by the way he held her that he wanted this. It was an act of intimacy, a feeling she could sense - something he'd deprived himself of for too long. At least, that's how it felt when he wasn't trying to talk.

"I'm not that guy," Andy said, again trying to pull away.

"What guy?" Sloane asked, her tongue running up his neck toward his ear. She gave him a nibble, and he shivered.

"The kind of guy who sleeps with a woman he's just met," Andy said softly.

She felt his pants grow tight under her and she knew he didn't want to believe that about himself.

"Oh, don't worry about that. I'm that type of girl, when the occasion calls for it," Sloane said, just as softly.

She bit his earlobe again, ever so slightly.

It helped that he wasn't just another slobbering idiot. It further endeared her toward him; made her want him. Ordinarily, she'd have to fake these types of arousals. His denial of what was happening compelled her to take it as far as she could.

"Can we just k–keep talking?" he stuttered.

"No more talking," she quietly commanded.

"I'm more interested in a long-term relationship."

"I don't care."

"With someone I can form a connection with."

"I'm only blowing through this place."

"So maybe we should just stay friends."

"We are friends, Andrew."

"Yeah, exactly."

"Friends with benefits." She pulled his shirt free of his pants and ran her hands against his taut stomach – not what she'd anticipated but delight lit her nerves all the same.

"Nope. You don't get it," he whispered into the hair behind her ear.

"Let go. Become one with me."

"I'd rather not at this time."

"Don't you think I'm beautiful?"

Her grip on his lapels loosened. *I don't get it...* He took her face into his hands, cupping either side of her cheeks. Sloane's hands stilled against his chest as her brain scrambled to understand. They were both out of breath. She avoided his gaze.

"You're very beautiful, but I'm not looking for this type of thing right now," Andy said, his voice hitching as the warmth of his palms fed into the heat of her passion.

"Please, it's been so long for me. Hasn't it been long for you, too?" Sloane returned.

"That feels overly personal."

"Good, let's get very personal." Her gaze returned to his.

"I want something deep and meaningful. Not superficial," he said.

"Does this feel superficial?" Sloane slid her arms around Andy and put every ounce of passion and longing into a kiss. She was confused about his restraint and couldn't be clearer with her intentions. Any other man would jump off a cliff for a chance to be with her. She pulled away from him and looked around anxiously, attempting to find an answer to this conundrum.

This strange man who had smiled at her as she walked into the dining hall now pushed her away. She didn't know what she could do to get him into her good graces, to gain the sort of control she knew she could have over a man.

Sloane couldn't believe she'd put herself in this position in the first place. She was there on business; this wasn't an occasion for recreation. There was no need for this man or any other for satisfaction; she had enough poor experience to know that for sure. All she ever needed was for them to listen; and they did. Even if they weren't conscious of what she was saying; completely mesmerized by her beauty, they still abided her commands. She only ever took it further than a simple seduction when the need arose.

Andy would be of good use to her, but only if he cooperated. If he wouldn't cooperate, she'd have to manipulate, and the only way she could do that was by knowing who he really was and why he did the things he did.

"Fine," Sloane said, as she nuzzled into his neck.

She gave him one last shiver with the touch of her breath and slid free of their embrace, releasing his jacket. He fell on his elbows in the sand. She still straddled him with her arms crossed, feeling strangely exposed.

"Thank you. Now, can we just talk about this? I really like you. So maybe down the line we can try this again," Andy said.

Sloane merely looked down at him with flared nostrils and a raised eyebrow – a type of calm that came before a storm.

"What's wrong?" Andy asked, sitting back up and trailing his fingers along the side of her face. He shook his head and gently moved a lock of hair from her shoulder.

Sloane remained silent.

"Come on, tell me. If you're embarrassed, it's okay. We can forget this ever happened."

She gave him nothing.

"Really? The silent treatment? I think we need to be together a little longer than twenty minutes before you're allowed to give me the silent treatment."

She could tell he was confused and watched sweat bead along his forehead. Then, she started counting.

"Ten."

"Ten what?" Andy asked.

"Nine."

"I don't understand."

"Eight."

"Why are you counting down?"

"Seven."

"Listen, we can talk about this." Andy tried to get up, but she wouldn't let him move.

"Six."

"Come on. You're starting to scare me."

"Five."

"Okay, okay."

"Four."

"All right, that's enough. I won't have any more of this. You're going to stop–"

"Three."

"I'm sorry. I'm so sorry. Whatever you want, we'll do."

"Two."

"Stop it already. I'm not going to sleep with you."

Sloane went silent again. She knew Andy had no idea what it meant; good or bad.

Sloane reached behind her. Andy winced as she brought her hand back into view. She produced a business card. She tucked the card in his inside jacket pocket. As he fumbled around for it, she rose.

"What's this?" Andy asked.

"You passed the test," she said.

"What?" He was clearly dumbfounded.

As she stood over him, he laid back on the sands of the dirty beach in the cold, wet night. She'd dropped him hard, and she could tell it affected him.

He glanced at the card and looked at the phone number before flipping it over to read her name.

In bold, capitalized letters spelled one word:

SLOANE.

"Call me," she said.

Sloane grabbed her stilettos and walked away into the night.

6

SLOANE

A knock roused Sloane, which she ignored. Whoever it was would not receive her attention. She didn't expect or want to be bothered while she stayed in her gorgeous hotel suite.

The knock came again, and again she ignored it.

"Can't you read the fucking sign. It says 'Do Not Disturb.'" Sloane groaned.

The annoying knock persisted. Sloane squinted over at the bedside clock. 10:43 a.m.; far too early for her to be awake.

"This is bullshit." She groaned again, dragging herself out of bed.

Sloane put on a robe and went to the door only when it became clear the knocking would continue until answered. She opened the door without checking the peephole.

"Robbie, can't you read? I don't want to be bothered," Sloane said angrily. When she looked up, she nearly pissed herself.

"Shit."

"Hello, Sloane," the shorter of three men standing there said.

Sloane tried closing the door but the other two men thrust it open.

"What the fuck do you want?" Sloane asked as the men forced their way into her suite.

"Is that any way to greet old friends?" the short man asked, pulling his cuffs straight as he strode across the threshold not even glancing toward Sloane.

He admired his reflection in the mirror by the door, his dark complexion contrasting Sloane's porcelain hues. He took off his black hat and brushed his short black hair forward to even it out.

"I don't want to talk to you right now, Jackson," Sloane said. "And I know you always do the talking. You aren't good for anything else, anyway."

"I don't really give a shit who you want to talk to. Do you really think we can't find you wherever you go?"

Sloane panicked. Slyly she placed her hands behind her back. To them it seemed she was in control, but in reality it allowed her fingers to fidget as she tried to get out of this situation.

This was not how she wanted the day to begin; so early in the morning — and to have to face-down former clientele. Her business with Jackson had concluded, and for whatever reason they were there it could not be a good one. She glanced at the large window overlooking the coastline outside and considered her chances of survival if she leapt out.

This was bullshit she didn't want to deal with anyway. After a rather brief consideration, she thought it foolhardy and redoubled her focus on talking her way out of Jackson's most apparent gripe.

"Yeah, pretty much. Hey, Juan. Hey, Carl." Sloane saw no

reason to be impolite to the ass-hat's flunkies.

Juan was clearly a Japanese man. Sloane wasn't sure why they called him Juan. Carl was in fact Hispanic. She didn't get why he was called Carl, either. Both were large, heavyset men filling out dark leather jackets. She assumed they wore the jackets because they'd seen one too many mob-movies and figured it was how tough guys dressed. She thought it made them look like cocks, and she rolled her eyes at their idiotic ensemble.

"Well, you're wrong," Jackson said.

"Who squealed?" Sloane put her hands on her hips.

Her gaze darted from face to face trying to uncover what might have occurred to have her location unveiled prematurely. Her heartbeat rose every moment they stood in her Presidential Suite. Juan and Carl's dumbfounded faces, as she might have suspected, gave her no clues.

"Why does someone have to snitch for us to find you? Maybe we're really clever," Jackson said. A smug, knowing smile crept across his face.

"I'm not stupid. Who ratted me out?"

"No one betrayed you. I promise."

"Come on, tell me. You had to have hurt someone for them to have sold me out. Who did you do it to?"

"Okay, I'll tell you. But you won't like it."

"Don't tell me it was Rebecca."

"It was Rebecca."

Sloane's heart stopped for a second. She'd taken Rebecca under her wing, teaching her all the ways to take things from others and make it seem as though it were their idea all along. Rebecca was still young and impressionable when Sloane left her. Her sudden grief manifested into a torrent of rage.

"You son-of-a-bitch. I will cut your fucking head off." Sloane's eyes widened with a fury that turned her once flawless face into a demon's.

Jackson laughed.

"It's not funny. You know I had a connection with her," Sloane said.

"It wasn't Rebecca. I lied." Jackson nearly doubled over, holding his stomach as another snicker escaped.

"Who was it then?"

"It was Georgie." He gasped through a breath and stood straight.

"Oh. Fuck Georgie."

"I know, right?"

"Did you make him suffer?"

"'Course we did. He gave you up way too quickly."

"Good. Do you guys want to sit?"

"Nah. We aren't staying long."

"What's the problem? I thought our business was done."

Sloane turned her back to him. She walked over to the coffee machine and fiddled with the buttons to turn it on. She needed something hot and strong right about now.

"It was, until we tried using the product."

"Good stuff." Sloane turned back to Jackson.

"The demo was great. The rest of it, not so much," he said, shrugging, his eyes conveying irritation.

"What?" Sloane cocked her head and fluttered her eyelashes.

"One of my guys got thrown through a wall." Jackson twitched.

"He didn't use it right. Not my problem." Sloane's frown grew with mounting frustration every passing moment.

"We've already made the return."

"No refunds."

"Tell that to your supplier."

"This is bullshit," Sloane spat.

"We were guaranteed our money back." Jackson's voice rose.

"And?"

"Where is it?"

"How should I know?"

"They said you'd have it. So either you pay us back, or–"

"Or? Or what? You're going to kill me?"

"Nah. I won't lay a finger on you. But your people aren't going to be too happy you aren't facilitating all that good."

"The fuck do any of you know about what I have to do on a daily basis to keep you all happy?"

"Not my problem. I'm just here to collect. Not to enforce."

"I don't have the money on me."

Jackson pulled out his phone.

"What are you doing?" Sloane asked.

"What's it look like I'm doing? I'm making a call," Jackson replied.

"Who are you calling?"

"A pizza place."

Sloane wasn't amused.

"I'm calling your people. You know what happens next," Jackson said.

"That won't be necessary."

"So, you got my money?"

"No, of course not."

"Then I'll just tell your people you can't deliver. You can take it up with them."

"Okay, that's enough." Sloane reached for Jackson to stop.

"Not until I get my money."

"I can get it for you." She put her hands up in surrender.

"How? When?"

"I was already working on something out here. Whatever I get from that, I'll give to you."

"No, no, no. You will give me exactly what you owe me."

"What I'm doing isn't that big. Let this be a down payment."

"No. I want my money. I got stuff I need to do, and I can't waste my time dealing with you. I ain't a loan shark."

"Fine. I'll figure it out."

"Good girl. Now, when you gonna pay me?"

"I should have your money by the end of the weekend."

"Good." Jackson looked at Juan and Carl. He nodded to them, and they moved around the suite. "This is a nice hotel room," Jackson remarked. "Shame."

"What?" Sloane asked.

She got her answer.

Juan and Carl smashed the television to the ground. They punched through the paintings on the walls. They tore up the pillows and cushions on the couches. They snapped the dining room table in half. They broke vases, crystal-stemware, glasses, and anything else they could get their hands on.

To finish the job, they punched holes in the walls. Jackson called them off after a while, and Juan and Carl headed for the door.

"I'll be seeing you around, Sloane." Jackson left the door wide open as he and his goons left.

Sloane stood still, as still as she had during the destruction of her suite. She understood what they were doing. They were making her feel uncomfortable. They didn't care how much it would cost to fix the suite, and they knew she could talk her way out of paying for it anyway. It was them she couldn't talk around. There was no clever sell she could make to get them off her back. She would have to face them or deal with her employer. If Jackson had any decency, he'd have just taken out the revolver she knew he had and got on with it.

She moved to the couch and sat, exhausted. Sloane took stock of what just happened. Then, she stood back up. Now was not the time to rest. She had work to do. And she knew just who to go to.

7

ANDY

Andy couldn't get his mind off Sloane. His jaw had hung open to the point of exhaustion, and yet it stayed open even as the waves continued to crash and his clothes grew damper seated on the beach the night before. She'd played games with him, and he never got the chance to learn the rules. Left on the shore was everything of his old life; every thought, every idea, beached by the tidal force that was Sloane.

Andy wanted more of her, or at least he thought he did, not really knowing what he wanted; unsure if he should call her or pack a bag and flee the country.

Either way, Andy would always have her on his mind. Every thought would be of the peculiar, mysterious, captivating woman who knew what she wanted, and more importantly, how to get it.

Andy could never be with her as just a simple accountant

with a simple life. Sloane was an elemental force. She moved so quickly, so confidently. Confidence which eluded him. Andy was nothing like her, and he was envious. He'd never be able to keep up with her, of that he was sure. Not because of what he knew about her, but of what he knew about himself.

Andy had lain on the beach for a solid hour, completely perplexed as to what had happened. When he'd finally regained feeling in his testicles, he'd slowly stood up, dusted himself off, and headed home.

The walk was three miles from the beach, but with Andy's mind still on Sloane, it felt like a jaunt up the driveway.

At home, Andy pulled off his clothes, took a long cold shower, and then laid on his bed. He didn't fall asleep. Instead, he stared at the ceiling, thinking of nothing but Sloane.

Andy's waking dream of Sloane was of the first moment she graced his vision with her gorgeous movie-star face. Of her slamming open the doors of the Country Club and striding in as though she were the sovereign. Her lavender scent still lingered on Andy well into the next day. A scent he would miss soon after it faded.

The next morning, Andy drove himself to work all the while his mouth still agape. He slumped into the empty offices of Allied Accounting a zombie. Walking into the conference room, he sat for half an hour still transfixed on Sloane. Only when Jerry and his father, Frank, joined him did Andy break his funk, and he described what transpired the night before.

"She is beautiful. She is entirely perfect," Andy said.

"He's right, Frank. She was great," Jerry piped up.

"Well, what is this beautiful creature's name?" Frank asked.

Andy's father was as mild-mannered as his son, maybe

even more so. His outlook on life was nowhere near as cynical as Andy's, but not as naively-optimistic as Jerry's. Frank was a realist. He was almost seventy years old, and Andy knew he couldn't afford to be anything but realistic about things.

"Sloane," Andy said, deflating as he did.

"Sloane?" Frank asked, incredulously. "What kind of name is that?"

"It's a regular name, sir," Jerry said.

"Okay. If you say so. Well, I'm happy for you, son. She sounds like a great gal."

"Yeah, but a little strange," Jerry said.

"Strange? What do you mean strange?" Frank tilted his head.

"Maybe not strange. Aloof?"

"Aloof?"

"Eccentric."

"Eccentric?"

"Yeah, eccentric."

Andy rolled his eyes as one continued to parrot the other. "Stop repeating each other."

"What makes her so strangely, aloofly, eccentric?" Frank asked.

"Aloofly?" Andy frowned.

"You know what I mean."

"She wanted me."

"That's great."

"Not great." Andy rubbed his face and combed his hair with his hands making it stand up. "I mean she wanted me, wanted *me*. If you know what I mean."

"I think I do."

"This is such a weird conversation to have with my dad."

"What's weird about it?"

"I think Andy's trying to say this Sloane lady wanted to fuck him," Jerry explained.

"Jesus, Jerry!" Andy cried.

"Oh, I see," Frank said.

"But I didn't. Because I don't even know her. I mean, I literally just met her last night."

"Good for you, son. Take things slow. Especially after– Well, you know why."

"Yeah, I do."

"Now what?" Frank asked.

"I don't know. On one hand, she's incredible. On the other hand, she's absolutely certifiable."

"That's not necessarily a bad thing, huh, Andy?" Jerry joked. "Especially in the sack."

"Damn it, Jerry. If we had an HR department, I'd be reporting you to them right now." Andy slammed his hands on the conference table, surprised by the intensity of his reaction.

"I'm sorry, Andy. I'm just trying to be relatable."

"Here's a tip: stop trying."

"Got it."

Frank leaned forward. "Don't worry about Jerry. What about this woman? Did you get her number?"

Andy pulled out the business card. "Yeah. She gave me this."

"That's a good sign, so far."

"I should call her, right?"

"Of course."

"But she's insane."

"Don't put yourself in a dangerous situation. Be sensible."

"On the other hand, a little bit of danger could be good for me."

"Atta-boy. Live a little."

"Unless she's way too dangerous, and it gets me killed."

"No one's going to hurt my boy," Frank said grabbing a nearby file and thumbing through it.

"She tried to have sex with me on the beach. In the middle of the night. Out in the open."

"That is very odd."

"But it was also exhilarating." Andy leaned back as far as the office chair would allow as he stared at the flickering overhead lights.

"You should call her. That's final, Andy. If this woman is half as remarkable as you say, then she is also incredibly intelligent. She must see how great you are as well. You deserve to be happy, and if this woman can do that for you, I say you go for it. You're a catch, and any woman would be lucky to be with you."

"You're right, Dad. I'm going to call her."

Andy picked up a nearby phone and dialed the number from the business card.

"That won't be necessary," a posh, British-accented voice rose from the doorway of the meeting room.

"Sloane." Andy stood up and moved toward her nearly dragging the phone from the table before he realized what he was doing. He awkwardly placed the receiver back on the base upside down.

"Can we talk? It is extremely important we talk right away," Sloane asked.

"Yes, of course. Are you okay?"

Andy was concerned. He didn't expect to see her so soon. That, and she seemed different than the night before. He watched her scan the conference room before taking a minor glance toward Frank and Jerry. Something seemed off about her. He was curious to find out what could possibly be the reason for the pleasantly unannounced visit.

"No, Andrew. I desperately need your help," Sloane said, her eyes first averting, then locking with his gaze.

Andy nearly melted when she said his full first name.

"Come on. We can talk in my office."

Andy escorted Sloane through the firm to his office,

leaving Jerry and Frank alone in the meeting room. As Andy closed the doors to the conference space his father pronounced his final thoughts on Sloane:

"Forget everything I said earlier," Frank said. "That woman is a knockout. Andy's got no chance with her."

8

ANDY

Sloane plunked down on Andy's desk silently simpering as he closed the door behind him. She sat with her legs crossed, balancing her black stilettos on her toes, bobbing her foot as she waited for him. As Andy walked to his desk, his eyes were drawn from her delicate foot, up to her pearl-white skirt doing little to hide her long, slender legs. His eyes traced their way up to her matching pearl-white, low-neck blouse and her considerable cleavage. Then he followed the curve of her body to her long neckline; the same neck that marked him with lavender the night before. The same scent of which he wanted more.

His eyes moved along the perfectly sculpted bone structure of her face. Her vibrant dark-red lipstick puckered out, almost inviting him in for another kiss. Then his eyes finally met her's, shrouded in a smoky shadow.

Their gazes locked.

He stopped in his tracks. Bashing his leg into the metal

table momentarily brought him back down to earth. He loosened his tie to get some circulation.

Sloane sat upright, the perfect model of a pageant contestant, her eyes locked forward. Andy sat at his desk, but she never turned to look at him. It was as if the moment they locked eyes never occurred, and when it had, she had simply looked through him. All he saw was the back of her head.

Andy knew exactly what she was doing. She looked stunning, and she knew it. He wasn't a complete moron. Clearly, she was trying to seduce him again, to get him to do or say anything she wanted.

And it worked.

Andy remained helpless against her spell, especially now after he'd sobered up. He no longer had the courage to be a charming imbecile. And he felt stupid he hadn't slept with her the night before. Even if it would've been foolish if he had.

"Nice office. Very quaint," she said.

"Thanks, I think."

Andy wasn't sure what game Sloane played. He didn't understand why she was so interested in him. Unsure what he could possibly do for her, he considered what it could have been. It wasn't that he was particularly handsome, funny, or intelligent. Put simply, he was just a normal guy, and her possible intentions perplexed him.

"What's wrong?" Andy asked.

"Oh, nothing. Just a minor matter of life and death."

"Right. So, it's simple, then?"

Sloane's casual tone faded. What he thought was a gag was actually far more dire. She was serious.

"Can I tell you something I've never told anyone before in my entire life?" Sloane asked, her voice becoming softer.

"What is it?" Andy asked, leaning forward, fully engaged.

Her voice grew low and quiet. She had something to say

that she dare not say above a whisper. It only made whatever she said next that much more intriguing.

"I think I've fallen for you, Andrew."

The sentiment was genuine, or at least she made it seem as much. But there was something off Andy couldn't quite put his finger on. He wasn't sure how to figure out what was bugging him about her. Though what she said seemed honest, skepticism remained his only ally.

"We haven't even known each other for twenty-four hours. And I thought you had more pressing matters. We should probably share a meal together first before we even talk about who's fallen for whom."

"Oh, I don't eat," Sloane said matter-of-factly.

"Lunch?"

"Anything."

"At all?"

"I nibble. I don't eat."

"What are you, a vampire?"

Sloane laughed. "You're so funny."

"Wait, seriously?"

"Andrew, I need your help with something."

"With what?" Impatience edged his voice. He needed to know what someone like her got into when the sun went down and all the meek folk shuttered themselves in for the night.

Sloane pulled out a large manila envelope from her off-white Yves Saint Laurent purse. She held it for him. Andy stood and took it, then sat back down as he opened it.

The envelope held tax documents, bank transaction notifications, other forms, and a hand-written letter from a man named Enrique.

Andy didn't understand. "What is all of this?"

"My problem," Sloane said breathlessly.

"I don't get it."

Andy was more than confused, he was let down. This was

it. A manila envelope full of forms; the type of business he dealt with all the time. Nothing unique or out of the ordinary. All she'd handed him was his every day, simple, boring, draining life. Was this all he was good for? Was this all she could offer him?

"Tell me what you don't understand, and I'll try to explain," she said.

"I understand you're out of money, and you owe more than you ever had in taxes. And some guy named Enrique took your life savings."

"Yes."

"I don't understand how I'm supposed to help you."

"Enrique was an old lover of mine. That's why I'm here in Riders Bay. Last I heard, he was here."

"I've never heard of an Enrique."

"It doesn't matter. They called me at my hotel suite this morning and told me they have him now."

"Who's they?"

"The ones who are after me."

"The government after your taxes?"

"No, the mob."

"The mob?" Andy asked incredulously.

"That's right. They've been following us. Enrique was into something with the mob. He was a hitman for them. That's how we met. He was supposed to assassinate me."

"What?" Andy's eyes widened, and his pulse quickened. *This is more like it.*

"That's right. I was working with the Feds as an undercover informant. I learned all sorts of intel for them about the mob. They were going to bring down the whole criminal organization, the same organization that killed my dear baby sister, Tiffany. I wanted revenge, you see. Against the monsters who killed my innocent, disabled sister. She was born paralyzed from the ears down."

"That's so sad."

"The mob sent Enrique to kill me when they found out I was about to testify in open court. All four hundred members of the mob would have received the death penalty."

"I see why they would want you dead."

"Anyway, Enrique couldn't do it. He couldn't pull the trigger. Instead of killing me, we made furious love, right there, on the edge of a cliff. Literally, the edge of a cliff."

"That sounds super dangerous."

"He wore protection. Then we ran away and the mob was after us both. We moved from town to town for ten years. Then one night, he just left. With all my money, which I had stolen from the mob."

"And the mob found you? Why haven't they killed you?"

"After the failed assassination attempt, the prosecutor's case fell apart. The mob was acquitted on all charges. I was no longer a threat to their organization. When they found me, I told them if they killed me, they'd never see a dime of their money again. So, for obvious reasons, they kept me alive. Except, I lied, Andrew. I don't have their money, and when they discover this, they will kill me, and literally everyone else in this town."

"Wait, what?"

"That's right, Andrew. They're that vicious. They would burn this entire town to the ground just to make a point. They must be stopped."

"How?"

"We get them the money."

"No, I get that. But how? I don't have any money."

"Yes, but you do the taxes of all the people who do – all of the richest people in this town. Which must be a considerable amount, is it not?"

"Yeah, but–"

"I knew as soon as I saw you that you were the only one who could protect me. The only one who could save me."

Andy looked at Sloane. Part of him was trying to figure

out if she told the truth, the other part was confused as to why he still only saw the back of her head.

He knew just of what Sloane was asking. She wanted him to steal from his clients. There was no way for her to know his only clients were the ones with the lowest sums of money. He didn't want her to know that.

To tell her he couldn't help would be a death sentence to his chances with her. And, there was the other dilemma of him not wanting to commit fraud for a woman he hardly knew. Even if he did have rich clients, it would go against everything he stood for to rob them. Even if a little robbing was the type of swift kick in the ass the wealthy of Riders Bay required. It was wrong, yet, it would only hurt those in his town who barely cared about anyone but themselves.

It could be a type of karmic justice... As his thoughts battled between what was ethical and his cathartic need for retribution against those like Thomas Rosenbaum, he snapped back to the reality that people like Rosenbaum weren't apart of his clientele.

He needed to buy himself some time to think. To think of a way to keep her close to him and his chances with her alive.

9

SLOANE

Sloane didn't need to look Andy in the eye to know he'd bought her story. It came from her, and she had a trustworthy face. However, she wondered why she hadn't turned yet to flash her emerald eyes at him to seal the deal. She was there, at the goal line. She knew she had him, she would have looked at anyone else; it was, after all, her face he'd have the opportunity to gaze upon. Or, as others called it: the most beautiful thing they had ever had the fortune of looking upon. Once she was gone from them, all-purpose ceased to exist, and all hope in the world was lost.

So, of course, she knew he'd believe her. Still, Sloane hesitated for another long moment before turning her neck to gaze upon Andy's dumbfounded expression. She rested her chin on her shoulder and forced herself to bat her long, luscious eyelashes. Then, she flashed her pearly whites at him. She felt strange about it. She'd done this so many times before, but now it felt different.

"What do you say? Will you help me?"

Andy looked down at the letter from Enrique, which Sloane had written.

"He's got really nice handwriting," Andy remarked.

"Enough about the past. What about our future?"

Andy looked up from the letter and into her deep, captivating green eyes. After another moment, he stood up and paced around the room before turning to her.

"I think I can help you," he said, finally.

"You can? That's splendid." Sloane clasped her hands together.

"Except, I'm going to have to move some things around."

"Okay, get to moving."

"It's just, I'm not sure she'll accept that."

"Well, she's going to have to. Whomever she is."

He sighed and ran his hand through the hair at his temples. "I still love her." Pain laced his voice.

"Excuse me?"

"I can't lie to you, Sloane. I'm in love with another woman."

Sloane jumped from the desk and slapped Andy across the face. "How could you?"

"I still want to help you. But I'll also need your help."

"I don't know if I should."

Sloane looked away to hide her bewilderment. Her eyes widened. *How did this turn around so fast?* It was all so terrible. Everything was falling apart: her plans, her tested techniques. She was getting everything wrong, and she wasn't sure she could salvage this debacle. Sloane might just thrash herself to the ground in frustration. It baffled her. She had been flawless in her execution, and yet Andy only wanted to go through with his *thing* instead. *Am I losing my touch?* Sloane shook off her self-doubt. She knew what she was doing. This could be salvaged. She would force it to be so if necessary.

"Who is she? Do I know her?" Sloane asked turning back around after she composed herself.

"Well, no. You don't know anybody. You came here yesterday."

"Don't play games with me, Andrew."

"She's my ex-wife."

"Your ex-what?"

"We were married for five years, then she left me. Said I was too boring. That I wasn't living up to my considerable potential. That I never took out the trash."

"How miserable."

"I know."

"I don't understand. How can I help?"

"My ex is extremely jealous, one of the many things I love about her. That, and her need to control every aspect of my life."

"I understand that."

"If she– No. It's a stupid idea."

"No, no. Tell me."

"Okay. But if you think it's a stupid plan, we won't do it."

"Just tell me."

"Pretend to be my fiancé, and then she'll want to come back to me."

"That's a stupid plan."

This became an unnecessary detour Sloane desperately wanted to avoid at all costs. Unfortunately, Andy didn't seem too eager to cooperate despite being told a complete fabrication and having no reason to trust her anyway. She didn't have time for this, yet she saw no other choice but to go through with his harebrained scheme.

"Here me out," Andy began. "First, we pretend to be together, happy and gay."

"Those are the same thing," Sloane returned.

"Then we kiss in front of her, and show her how happy I am without her – I mean, with you."

"I see." She rolled her eyes.

"She'll get so jealous she might even try to fight you, and that's how we'll know we've got her."

"I don't see how that would be okay for me." She shook her head and frowned.

"She'll be running back to me, and by then you'll have your money, and you'll be on your way. Your way out of town, never to return again, no matter what."

Sloane's eyes darted, not trying to find anything in particular, except for where this man-child came off kicking her out of town. She was a respectable lady. When it was time to run her out, it would be with a proper angry mob, not a single dope.

But there was something else in his tone which made her uncertain. On the one hand, it did make perfect sense to want her as far away from others as possible. She was aware of what she would do to unwitting souls; it was why she exclusively swindled from the unwitting. On the other hand, she wasn't sure that was truly what he wanted. That perhaps he was only saying what he thought she wanted to hear. It made her more curious to his real motivations.

"I don't know. Your plan is sort of silly. And I know all about being deceitful. Perhaps if we workshop the idea a little–"

"There's no time. She's coming right now." Andy frantically checked his watch.

"What?"

"That's right."

"What? Here?"

"That's right. Here. Soon."

"In your office?"

"Yep."

"I need more time. More time to think about this. More time to prepare. More time to check my makeup."

Sloane didn't want this. The ordeal spiraled from bad to

worse and it made her sweat. She hated being sweaty. It was an involuntary reaction to untamable situations. She didn't believe in such things as untamable situations. Not for her anyway. Sweating was for the weak and those who performed manual labor, which were other things she hated.

"Sorry. We don't have that kind of time. What will it be? Yes or no?" Andy asked.

Sloane was dumbstruck. This wasn't at all what she'd had in mind, and she certainly didn't have any time for this. She was on a tight schedule, and Andy was being inadvertently inconvenient. Once again though, she begrudgingly respected him for his unintentional countermove to a game he wasn't even aware he played.

"Do we have a deal?" Andy stretched out his hand. Sloane didn't have a choice. It was either go along with his poorly-conceived, idiotic plan to get back with his probably plain-looking ex-wife, or find some other way to get the money she owed Jackson and his people.

Sloane was out of options and out of time. "You scratch my back, I'll scratch yours type of deal?" Sloane asked, still trying to decide if he was worth the dwindling time she had left.

"That's right. So, are you in or are you out?"

Sloane had never been here before. She was the one who gave ultimatums. And already, in the span of only a few hours, she got shoved between a rock and a hard place. She hated the feeling, and therefore, she finally understood what her prey experienced before she swooped in for the kill, taking everything valuable.

It was karmic justice, she supposed. Though it felt like shit to be used, she sort of respected Andy for doing it to her so flawlessly. It was the perfect time and place. If she were in his place, she would have taken full advantage of the situation as well. She finally understood what it meant to get fucked.

"Fine," Sloane said, reluctantly. She reached out and shook

Andy's hand, firmly and furiously. When he pulled his hand away, he shook it off to alleviate some of the pain.

"Good, we have a deal," Andy said, through gritted teeth.

"Now what?" Sloane asked.

A knock at the door made her jump a little.

"Hello, Andy," a woman said, entering.

Andy caught Sloane off guard, pulling her into his embrace. Tenderly holding either side of her face he kissed her, moving her to his desk, leaning her over it. She knocked things down. Her heartbeat raced erratically. Sloane had never let something like this happen to her before, but was thrilled Andy pushed it to this. She wanted so badly to take him into her fully, but they had a sudden audience.

The mousey woman walked in. "Oh, I didn't know you had company."

Andy glanced up from kissing Sloane. Her lipstick stained his mouth. She gave a gasp for breath, and it took her a moment to regain her composure.

"Oh, hello, Karen," Andy said, moving from Sloane, creating a gulf between them she no longer wanted. "I didn't expect you so soon."

"It's two o'clock. Like every weekend. Who's your friend?"

"Sloane, this is ex, my Karen. Karen, this is fiancé, my Sloane. Err. I mean Sloane, this is Karen, my ex. And Karen, this is Sloane, my fiancé. You get what I'm saying."

"You're ridiculous," Sloane hurriedly said under her breath to Andy, before moving over to address Karen. "Yes, hello. I'm pleased to finally meet you. I feel we were just talking about you."

Sloane shook Karen's hand delicately and did a slight curtsy and bow. Andy frowned, perplexed. Karen merely smiled, seemingly impressed.

"I didn't know he was seeing anyone. I wish you would have warned me, Andy. I would have told her."

"Told who?" Sloane asked.

A young girl burst past Karen and ran over to Andy.

"Daddy!" the girl semi-toothlessly giggled as she hugged him. Her frizzy hair bobbed into Andy's face causing him to choke for a moment.

"You have a daughter," Sloane said as more of a realization than a statement. "Shit."

10

KAREN

Karen Teague had lived in Riders Bay her entire life and was as much a part of the town as the pot-holed streets and dilapidated public buildings. That morning, Karen drove her mid-sized SUV through the quiet streets of Riders Bay with Samantha in the backseat.

"Mommy, when can we go to the zoo again?" Karen didn't hear her daughter at first. She looked out at the foreclosure signs in all the storefronts she went to as a child. A profound sense of loss gripped her heart. She pushed back tears with the back of her hand as she passed another memory closed for business. With each boarded-up store, it was as though she lost her father all over again.

"I don't know, honey," Karen finally replied.

"I want Daddy to take me this time."

"Daddy can only see you during the weekends, and he's always so busy at work."

"I know."

Karen drove past a shop with a beat down sign: TEAGUE'S FLOWERS.

"Hey, look, it's your mommy's old store," Karen announced, as she wiped her nose.

"What kind of store is it?" Samantha asked.

"Well, it's closed now, but it was a flower shop. It used to be your grandpa's."

"Grandpa is an account."

"Accountant. And I mean your other grandpa. My dad. Grandpa Frank is your father's dad."

"Okay."

"He passed away before you were born. He left me his shop. I don't think I was as good as he was at running a store. But it was all for the best. If the store hadn't closed down, I wouldn't have met your father, and then you wouldn't be here."

"Can I get ice cream?"

"You have to ask your father." She didn't mean to snap at her daughter, but she always felt unsettled meeting with Andy. That awkward, queasy feeling in the pit of her stomach was why she didn't eat before meeting with him, certain she'd empty the contents of her breakfast on his shoes. Not as though she didn't think he deserved it, she just didn't like confrontation.

Every weekend, Karen brought Samantha to the offices of Allied Accounting, Andy's second home. To pay the alimony and child support, he was often at the office taking on as many extra clients during tax season as he could.

As despondent as Andy could be, he completely lit up when Samantha came around. Karen knew his daughter was the only thing keeping him sane.

She parked the SUV in the nearly empty, damp parking lot of the strip mall just in front of the Allied Accounting offices. She got Samantha out of her car seat, and her little girl hopped out of the vehicle and ran ahead through the office doors.

"Honey, wait up. Slow down," Karen called out as she hurried after her.

Samantha scurried through the empty office space to the conference room where she found Frank reading over some forms. Frank smiled as he hugged and put Samantha on his lap, asking how her week went. Karen absentmindedly walked to Andy's unusually closed office door and gave a cursory knock before entering.

Karen caught Andy in a compromising position, and yet it seemed as though he didn't care what anyone thought. Karen's eyes widened, and her mouth went dry. Her head moved in circles as she indecisively went from looking away from the display of affection to feeling she had no reason to look away in the first place. She was speechless and answered all of Andy's questions on autopilot as her brain whirled with a single question of its own: *Why didn't he ever do that with me?*

Samantha burst into the office past Karen as she ran over to Andy. Without a second thought, he picked her up and nuzzled her cheeks. Something in Karen wanted to yelp; some unconscious need to protect her daughter from the girl's own father. His lips were just on a stranger's and she didn't want him touching Samantha.

Karen, though, held her tongue and just as absentmindedly followed Andy out of his office to find a bigger space for them all to talk. They went to the conference room and took seats around the oval table.

"How's my girl?" Andy asked.

"We saw butterflies," Samantha said.

"You know your Uncle Jerry used to collect bugs," Jerry said.

"Why am I not surprised?" Karen refrained from rolling her eyes, but only just. She kept a very limited relationship with Jerry, allowing him to refer to himself as "Uncle Jerry," but only because he had nothing else tying him to the world. She wasn't even sure she ever learned his last name.

"Tell your father what else you saw this week," Frank prompted Samantha.

Frank was always kind to Karen, even during her marital troubles with his son and the subsequent divorce. He gave her a job as an office assistant when she was penniless after her business failed. She respected him and was still incredibly fond of him. He, in turn, had never been anything but loving.

Samantha sat on Andy's lap across from Karen. At the far end sat Frank, and, for some reason, "Uncle Jerry." Sitting overly close to Andy was the tall, leggy, blonde, well-postured, busty, sharply-dressed woman Karen had the unfortunate pleasure of bumping into while her ex-husband had her over his desk.

Karen forced herself to sit up straight in her chair.

"So how long has this been going on?" Karen asked.

"How long has what been going on?" Andy returned, with a frown.

"You and Miss – I'm sorry, I forgot your name."

"Her name is Sloane. And you remember it just fine because I told you her name twenty seconds ago."

"So, you know what I'm thinking? That's strange because I remember that being something you always accused me of doing."

Karen looked directly into Andy's eyes with fury. The entirety of their past together flooded back with tidal force. She wanted to list all the reasons he was a shit-head to her for the last half-decade. Wanting to start in reverse order from the moment he brought a strange woman into their daughter's life without even consulting her. Her nose flared in a way she knew he'd recognize.

Andy raised his voice, "Stop it. Not right now."

"But, I'm a mind reader, or at least I used to be. Now, my powers have transferred over to you."

"If you could read my mind, you'd know I want you to stop."

"Children, children. Please," Sloane interjected. "I know things are very new and very tense for everyone. Let us allow for cooler heads to prevail."

Karen looked away, both embarrassed and annoyed. She felt like a child being told to calm down or she'd be sent to the Principal's office. Immaturity coated her like sticky honey pushing her to blame Andy for it. She couldn't have a conversation with him, she thought she never could. Anytime they tried, it turned into a petty argument. It made her feel stupid. Sloane, though, was apparently also level-headed, sophisticated, and British. And probably rich as well, by all appearances.

"You didn't answer my question, Andy," Karen said, still unwilling to look at anyone.

"I don't want to answer it," Andy said.

"You have to."

"Why?"

"Because we have a daughter, and you can't bring strange women into her life. No offense."

Sloane waved her off. "None taken. It's perfectly reasonable for you to know my intentions."

"And they are?"

"We have a sort of partnership arrangement. I didn't want to meet you or your young child so soon, or at all."

Sloane looked over at Andy with a sideways glance. Karen detected more to the look than a simple glance between lovers. Something else was going on, something that had nothing to do with a hapless idiot getting with a beautiful blonde. Then Karen second-guessed herself, not sure if she was seeing this as a result of her onset of childish behavior.

"This is another of your ill-advised, poorly thought-out ideas, isn't it?" Karen asked.

"Ladies and gentlemen, the mind reader," Andy quipped.

Karen didn't want this. She didn't want to argue or to meet her ex-husband's new, more beautiful, girlfriend.

"You know, I knew a mind reader of sorts when I lived in Marrakesh for six months." Sloane glanced at her perfectly manicured nails. "She was a wonderful fu–"

Sloane stopped short as she locked eyes with Samantha.

"–person."

"Nice save," Andy remarked.

Sloane merely scowled and pursed her lips in response, apparently holding herself back from cursing in front of his daughter.

"Do you have any kids?" Karen asked.

"Oh, God no," Sloane scoffed.

Karen sat there quietly. The beat lasted a full minute before Sloane broke the silence.

"Honey, would you be a darling and take your baby-child out for a walk or something? Perhaps for ice cream," Sloane asked.

"Ooh, ice cream!" Samantha exclaimed in delight.

"That sounds like a great idea," Karen seconded.

"Are you sure?" Andy asked.

"We're big girls. We'll be fine. And take the men with you. I want to talk to Karen, alone. Woman to woman. You understand."

"Sure."

Andy took Samantha and dragged out the drooling Frank, and Jerry, along with him. The conference room doors closed behind them. As they left, if felt as though Karen's past and her future were leaving her alone with a stranger for the rest of her life. Her heart broke; suddenly her ex-husband and father to her child, whom she once loved dearly, was moving on. She thought the day would come when they each moved on from each other, but not so quickly and not with her left behind.

Karen needed to know. She needed to know for certain

what Andy being with Sloane signified, and what it would mean for her.

"Could you tell me something?" Karen asked, her voice suddenly desperate. "Is he happier with you?"

"My dear," Sloane said softly.

"Just tell me."

"My love."

"I need to know."

"Jesus, lady. Get a hold of yourself."

Karen's lip quivered, and she struggled to hold back tears. But they came anyway. Wet streaks stained her face and she quickly wiped them away. Her childish behavior toward Andy came with a reason; she still had feelings for him. Feelings that, whether she liked it or not, gave her some sort of purpose. For the longest time she thought Andy felt the same way, but now that time was over for good.

"I didn't know he was really done with me," Karen said.

"Sister!" Sloane commanded.

Karen snapped back to the room, her gaze locking onto Sloane's vivid, deep-green eyes.

"Yes?" Karen responded as mousy as ever.

"Let's not degrade ourselves by wasting our considerably more valuable time whining and whimpering over some poor man-boy," Sloane said sternly. Her eyes glistened with devious intent. "We have far more pressing matters to discuss."

11

SLOANE

Caught off guard by the sudden appearance of a micro-person, or a child as Sloane was told they were to be referred, her eyes widened and her heartbeat quickened. She had an overwhelming sensation to kick off her heels and run as fast as she could away from Andy and his mundane suburban life. Then she remembered that little ones were potentially harmless, and not to be feared. And she had no intention of losing her heels during her escape.

Andy covered the younger-version-of-an-adult's ears as Sloane let out a "shit" then led everyone to the conference room for space.

"What's going on?" Sloane asked Andy as they walked into the room. "Who is this?" She gestured to the child. "What is happening?"

"This is my daughter, Samantha," Andy replied.

"I don't understand."

"She's my kid with Karen, my ex-wife who you met ten seconds ago."

"You didn't tell me there would be little things involved."

Sloane panicked more than she ever had in her entire life. Andy's child reminded her of things she knew about herself: Her constant need for freedom, and how a child was the very embodiment of a lack of freedom.

"Is it really so shocking I could have a child?" Andy asked a little perturbed.

"How do I answer in the affirmative without insulting you?" Sloane asked cautiously.

"Never mind."

"How many more are there?"

"Just Samantha," Andy replied as he sighed in apparent frustration.

"Will there be any other miraculous surprises I should be aware of?"

"No. This is it."

"Good. We must hold onto the smallest of good fortunes."

Andy frowned. Sloane could only imagine his frustration by her confusion, but wasn't sure herself about any of this. Uncertain about following Andy from his office to the conference room, Sloane wanted to make some excuse and leave, but didn't. Fighting the urge to avoid sitting next to Andy with his little girl bouncing on his lap, the mite giggled, and Sloane relented. She didn't want to have to deal with Andy's "adorably" dressed ex-wife as they sat down across from each other at the oval table.

But she did anyway.

Though Sloane was unsure about what to do next, having successfully avoided this very type of situation her entire life, she decided to hide her shock as best she could and have some decorum around the offspring of the dope and his meek ex-wife.

"Hello, I'm Sammy," the little girl said.

"Hello, Samantha. I'm Slo–"

"I'm this many." Samantha held up five fingers.

"Good for you," Sloane replied.

"How old are you?" Samantha asked.

"A little over this many." Sloane held up five fingers as well.

"Are you and daddy getting married?" Samantha asked with some melancholy.

"God, I hope not," Sloane replied with a scowl.

Sloane wanted nothing to do with the stupid questions the little female asked. She wanted to put a gag in the girl's mouth to keep her quiet. Then again, she always wanted to put gags in everyone's mouths to keep them quiet, so it was nothing personal.

"Good. I don't like marriage," Samantha said as she rubbed her eye.

"I think we'll become fast friends, child." Sloane smiled.

Samantha laughed as Andy tickled her and asked how her week went. He grinned. In the short time Sloane had known Andy, it was the first time she saw him genuinely happy.

It wasn't what she'd expected, and as Andy kept glancing over to Karen, Sloane realized none of this was what she'd expected – to be used as a pawn in a love game, an angle in a love triangle she had no business nor interest of which to be apart.

The squabbles and arguments they engaged in right in front of their daughter gave Sloane mixed feelings. To get them to stop, she separated them, essentially placing them both on time out. The energy they spent fighting over frivolous non-events only made Sloane suspect more and more that Andy might have told her the truth. He might still have some love left for Karen. This was completely fine by Sloane; it made her part of the bargain that much easier. All she needed to do was push a little, and they'd be back together. Then she would have her money.

But the ridiculous argument persisted, pushing Sloane to the verge of boredom. She sent Andy off with the child, cleared the room of any other troubling, trifling riffraff, and focused all her attention on the mousy woman before her. It was important Sloane have the ex-wife alone with her for a little while. It had been a spell since she last had a meaningful conversation with a woman – perhaps less than a day. She wanted to get a better feel for what this town had to offer. This meek woman before her would spill everything; Sloane could tell.

Karen was so deeply unimpressive that Sloane nearly laughed at the poor woman. She looked down at Andy's ex, who was much shorter, analyzing her pink floral dress with yellow dandelions and a gray cardigan as drab. The tiny woman was cute though, but in an unassuming sort of way.

Sloane wanted to bop her small button nose and squeeze her light rosy cheeks. Her fair complexion was far too sunken and in great need of sunlight. But there was something else about Karen that Sloane hadn't noticed until further inspection. A sort of look in her eye.

At first, Sloane assumed sadness. Karen had been in a pitiful and miserable situation. Sloane felt depressed just simply looking at her; until she realized the look of sadness was really one of longing. Likely, for her failed marriage and her hopes to rekindle it.

The look only made Sloane pity the poor woman more. She realized then there was no hope of returning to the way things had once been for Andy and Karen. It didn't sadden her to see others' misfortune. In fact, she made a living causing the misfortune of others. But she normally left town long before she could witness their despair. This despair in Karen wasn't caused by her, and yet Sloane felt in some way guilty she wasn't doing anything about it. Or that she didn't want to and didn't have the time to. No springtime, sunlight love. Just the coldness of winter, the desolation and depression which came with pondering the events of the past, wondering what had gone wrong and what they could have done to prevent the catastrophe that was their lives.

In her travels, mostly avoiding people trying to get their money back from her, Sloane had met a score of individuals, many of whom had significant others. She preyed on those who were at their most vulnerable; those types of people were often alone even while married. The kind of desolation she saw in others, she now saw in Karen. Sloane's immediate impulse was to steal her bank account information, but decided against it suspecting it wouldn't be worth her time.

She wanted to help Karen in some small way. Sloane, though a miracle worker, wasn't a God. There was only so much she could do.

As Karen went on about Sloane and Andy, their current relationship status, and asking if he was truly happy now without her in his life, all Sloane heard was whining from a woman, and a mother, who should have been more powerful.

Karen looked away, on the verge of tears. The longing was there as she bit her lower lip and held her chin up to keep the tears from streaming down her face.

Sloane couldn't take it anymore, and more importantly, she couldn't stand to see such a potentially halfway-decent woman being so torn down by a barely halfway decent man. After she denied herself the urge to steal from the woman, Sloane felt an overwhelming need to uplift Karen. To let her know her capabilities. Sloane didn't recognize the emotion welling up inside of her to help those less fortunate, and worried she needed to see a doctor. Fearing this was some sort of pang of kindness, she repurposed her need to uplift into something more self-serving, which immediately calmed her down.

Then, there was the other matter pressing on Sloane's mind: the matter of time, which was running out.

The weak, unassuming Karen would be perfect for

Sloane's plan. To get her involved wouldn't be vital, and it certainly wouldn't be necessary, but if it took her out of her melancholy and rose her up, there would be no harm in it either.

"Karen, my dear, could you grab us those cups for a drink?" Sloane asked.

Karen nodded and moved over to the nearby pitcher of water.

"Oh no, my love," Sloane said, taking out a flask from her purse. "Just the cups will do for now."

Karen got two cups, brought them over to Sloane, and sat down. Into them, Sloane poured the contents of the flask.

"No, thank you. Not for me," Karen said.

"Dear, dear. There's a special place in hell for those who waste perfectly good scotch. And there's another place just as bad for those who drink alone when with company."

"I'm already in a special hell."

"I'm sure it's not so bad. There are other fish in the sea. Other birds in the sky. You'll get back on that horse, or some other helpful metaphor. Then all will be right again. You'll see."

"Easy for you to say. I mean, look at you." Karen took a sip.

"I always do. But certainly a woman like you must run this town in your own special way?"

"No," Karen replied, modestly.

"Oh, I'm sure of it. I could tell when I first saw you. You must have them lined up around the block, as they say."

"No." Karen shook her head, and Sloane poured her another drink.

"Tell me about yourself. Have you ever left Riders Bay, or does everyone just seem to stay here for life?"

"Yeah, I've lived outside of town before."

"What made you do it?"

"I don't know," Karen said reflectively, then took a sip. "I guess I felt a need to expand my horizons. So, I left town after high school to go to one of those big city colleges."

"Then what?" Pouring her another drink.

"It didn't work out. I left after two and a half years. It was all a little too hard for me, I guess."

"Didn't you have any friends?"

"Not really. I never got invited to any of those parties or study groups. It got kind of lonely."

"Then you came back?"

"My dad died. He was the reason I stuck it out for more than six months. We talked every week. We were all each other had. My mother died during childbirth." She took another sip.

"Sorry to hear that."

"Yeah. So, I came back after he died. I stayed and ran his shop instead of going back to school."

"What kind of shop?"

"A florist shop. Teague's Flowers. That's what it was called. I was going to keep it open. You see my dad, Albert, he never remarried. He stayed devoted to that shop, to me, and to my mother's memory. I was going to keep his legacy alive. It was going to be a beacon of success in Riders Bay. I wasn't going to let it become an afterthought." She held up the paper cup in triumph.

"So, what happened?"

"After three years I went out of business. I guess I had no business running a business."

Karen brought the cup down in defeat and stared at the whiskey.

"By the way, who does run this town?" Sloane asked.

"What do you mean?" Karen replied.

"What I mean is, this town is in terrible disrepair. Who have you all put in charge to fix it?"

"You mean like a mayor or something?"

"That's right. Who's the mayor?"

"We don't have one."

"Really?"

"Really. We haven't had an official running the town for decades. Heck, probably before I was even born."

"Unbelievable."

Sloane stood up and paced the room. She now saw clearly the avenue through which she would spring her plan into action. It would be easy, if she pushed the right people into submission. She would start with the pitiful woman sitting in the conference room with her.

"That's the problem with this society. This decadent, poor-feeding-the-rich society." Sloane threw her hands in the air.

"You're right. The Rosenbaum's basically run this place like their own personal country. They get whatever they want, whenever they want."

"And how about smooth roads?"

"They don't really care about that stuff."

"Store fronts that aren't all boarded up?"

"Nope."

"Working streetlights instead of ones that flicker if they happen to work at all?"

"Nope."

"Clean streets and beaches?"

"Nope."

"Renovated public areas?"

"Hell nope."

"And that's what I'm talking about. We live in this nation of haves and have-nots. And the haves have all tricked us into thinking we'll join them one day. Just mop my floor one more time, get my dry-cleaning, clean my toilets. Do my laundry. Do my yard work. Do all of it, not for the whole. Just for me. They aren't the haves, they're the *me*-s. Me first, me always," Sloane said with exuberance.

She marched around the conference room like a dictator.

Sloane would know, she'd dated a few. With her chin up, she only ever looked down her nose at Karen.

"'*And what about me?*' You may ask. '*What about you?*' They reply. Don't be selfish. Your child doesn't need me to pay for their crumbling school, for their broken-down jungle-gym, for their peace of mind. My money belongs to me. And while we're on the subject of *me*, get *me* another lemonade," Sloane ranted.

This got a rise out of Karen. She was hyper focused. Sloane could probably get the meek woman to join a cult by the way she nearly drooled at every sentiment, the last of her whisky forgotten.

"When will we learn there are far more of us than there ever will be of them?" Sloane's voice became a furious roar. "They have enough, and they won't ever need any more. We are legion, and we demand respect. We demand control of our destinies, to no longer suffer the indignity of living as servants for the few."

Karen was on the verge of applause. This was some of Sloane's best work. It was a shame she wasted it on single person.

"We must take back control of this town." Sloane stood still before Karen. This was her pièce de résistance. "We must demand accountability from all its residents, regardless of status. We must resume the way of life which brought us all to prosperity to begin with – and it certainly had little to do with doing someone else's chores for crumbs." Sloane towered above an awestruck Karen.

"How long have you lived in Riders Bay?" Karen asked.

"Never mind that now. The real question is what will we do next?"

Karen was speechless. "Uh–"

"Exactly. The last day of the gala is tomorrow. And tomorrow we make–"

A ringing from her purse cut Sloane off. She pulled out her

cell, read a text message, and hurriedly placed the phone back.

"Damn it!" Sloane exclaimed. "Finish my thought," she said impatiently.

"We'll hold a special election tomorrow for mayor to collect more taxes from the rich?" Karen suggested.

"No, no. That's stupid. We'll hold a fundraiser for a special election for mayor. Now, I have to go. Think about this, and spread the word. The Country Club, tomorrow. Bring your spirit, and your money. We will win the day," Sloane said as she quickly left the conference room, and a stunned Karen in contemplative silence.

12

ANDY

A ndy returned to the offices of Allied Accounting with his young daughter about an hour later. They'd taken the ladies' suggestion to get ice cream, spending their time eating it at a nearby park. The gloomy, misty drizzle kept them from spending more time at the unusually empty playground.

Most weekends, families brought their young children to play for a while. They spent the rest of their time going from shop to shop, perusing the new products in town. At first, Andy assumed it was the unseasonable weather keeping everyone at home. Then he thought about it a while longer.

Weekends on the main strip of Riders Bay had been empty for a while, maybe even years. Same went for the playground. No one had time to bring their kids to the park anymore. Everyone spent whatever time they had working another job. Most worked a second job as a maid or a cook for one of the wealthier residents. The commutes were convenient; most workers lived in modest homes sandwiched by massive properties with mansions. Most people were either working for their neighbor or were employing them.

Samantha was still covered in sticky residue from her chocolate ice cream. Andy held her hand as she licked off whatever chocolate remained on her fingers and palms.

Karen shook her head at Andy. "I'll clean her up," she said matter-of-factly, obviously perturbed.

"What happened with you and Sloane?" Andy asked.

"Nothing. Just girl-talk. Very, very strange girl-talk. Then she left."

"What did you guys talk about?"

"Nothing you'd understand. There are men here for you."

"What men?"

"Suited men. How should I know? They're talking to Frank and Jerry."

Andy nodded as Karen took Samantha to the restroom to clean her up. He moved through the office to find his father, Jerry, and the men in suits who'd come for him.

"It's very important we talk to your son, Mister Simmons," a fair-skinned man told Frank.

They stood in the middle of the empty office, apparently waiting for Andy to return. Both men were tall and stiff. They wore matching black suits with black ties. The suits looked cheap, and the men wearing them seemed overly grave. Andy knew something was wrong.

"I'm his son," Andy said as he approached.

"Andrew Simmons?" the second, dark-skinned man, clarified.

"Yes, that's me. How can I help you?"

"I'm Special Agent Russell, this is my partner, Special Agent Thompson," the second man said as they both showed badges to Andy. "We're with the Federal Bureau of Investigation."

"FBI?" Andy asked in shock.

"That is the abbreviated name of our organization," Special Agent Thompson said.

"I know. What's going on? Do I need a lawyer or something?"

"No, sir," Special Agent Russell said. "You aren't in any trouble."

"But you are a person of interest," Special Agent Thompson added.

"We've been looking for you all day. We believe you may be in danger."

"Danger. What do you think my son is involved in?" Frank asked.

"We believe he's met and is now under the dangerous control of a master con-artist," Special Agent Russell explained.

"What? Andy doesn't know any con-artists," Jerry said.

"Is there somewhere we can discuss this matter privately?" Special Agent Thompson asked. "For your own protection."

"Sure, we can talk in my office." Andy led them to the door.

Nervousness coursed through his veins. Pure anxiety racked him to the bone, and Andy did all he could to keep himself from shaking uncontrollably. He never had any sort of encounter with a member of law enforcement, and now he'd skipped all the way to federal agents. Andy had no idea what was going on, but he needed to put on a brave face if he hoped to make it through.

Frank stood up. "Wait, are you sure about this, Andy? You don't have to do any of this alone."

"It will be perfectly fine, sir," Special Agent Russell said.

"Dad, it'll be okay. This way." Andy opened the door to his office.

"Well, all right, son. We'll be in the conference room if you need anything."

"Thanks." Andy followed after the special agents who tried to make themselves comfortable as they sat on the cheap-excuse-for-office furniture. Andy closed the door and sat down across from them at his desk.

"Okay, what's going on?"

"You are being conned, Mister Simmons," Special Agent Russell said. "Or at least are an unwitting pawn in an elaborate scheme."

"Excuse me? I'm no one's pawn. That can't be the case at all."

"It's true," Special Agent Thompson said. "Have you been in contact with a woman known as Sloane?"

Andy's eyes widened. His stomach dropped and heart tightened. He didn't know how they knew of Sloane. He couldn't believe they were after a woman he was seeing, albeit, for such a short time.

"Based on your stunned silence, we'll assume you've met her," Special Agent Russell said. "We've received word from sources in Mogadishu, where she was last seen, that she's come to Riders Bay to engage in her next con."

"Mogadishu? In Somalia? Africa?" Andy asked.

"That's right. Mogadishu is in Somalia. Somalia is in Africa. Any other questions?" Special Agent Thompson replied.

"Yes. How can this be possible? Are you sure you don't have the wrong person? Why was she in Africa? What's her last name? Am I in danger? Why has she chosen me? Do you know what she's got planned? How am I supposed to be involved? How did you guys get here so fast?" Andy asked frantically.

"The Bureau gives us a company car, to answer your last question," Special Agent Thompson said.

"As for the rest of your questions, I fear we won't be able to answer any of them," Special Agent Russell said. "What we can tell you is she is quite resourceful. She is capable of telling incredible, most times fantastic tales that people always believe, no matter how ridiculous.

"The stories are often elaborate and tug at your heartstrings. In fact, we once had her cornered in Honduras. She escaped using only a thumb tack and a sob-story about her dying grandmother, an orphanage that was about to explode, and a rebel faction hoping to use the destroyed orphanage as a cover to attempt a coup d'état."

"Suffice it to say, we fell for it," Special Agent Thompson said. "But fool us once, shame on her. Fool us twice… it'll never happen, damnit!"

"Calm down, Thompson."

"Sorry. I'm in control. I'm breathing. Ten, nine, eight, seven, six, five, four, three, two… Okay, I'm good."

"Where were we?"

The special agents looked over at Andy to check if he was following along. Andy had since taken out a note pad, jotting down all the connections from Special Agent Russell's account of Sloane's story.

"Well, she hasn't told me any outlandish stories," Andy said as he looked up from what he was writing. "Only that she fell in love with a hitman sent to kill her, named Enrique."

"Sir," Special Agent Thompson began. "There is no Enrique. She sold you a story, too. Damnit! Why does everyone fall for this?"

"It has yet to be explained," Special Agent Russell replied.

"Just like Alaska."

Bewildered, Andy wondered what the hell they were talking about, or what could have happened in Alaska to freak them out so much. He couldn't figure out how an event in an American state was as unexplainable as Sloane.

"What happened in Alaska?" Andy asked.

"That's classified," Special Agent Russell said.

"Stay focused," Special Agent Thompson said. "Now, do you know where she is?"

"No, of course not. All she gave me was her–" A buzzing in his pocket cut Andy short. "Excuse me, gentlemen."

Andy pulled out his cell phone and read the text message.

[It's me dear.]

[Sloane.]

[The men in suits.]

[They're FBI.]

[Or so they say.]

"Mister Simmons," Special Agent Thompson said. "She's cooking up some kind of scheme in town. That's the only reason she would reveal herself so soon. We don't know why. But whatever it is, we've gotten word you are somehow involved."

"Me?" Andy asked in shock. "How can I be involved? Who told you this?"

"Don't worry who told us," Special Agent Thompson said. "Just know we've been hunting her down for years. She's been on the FBI's Dark List for over five years."

"What's a Dark List?" Andy asked.

"That's also classified," Special Agent Russell said.

[Blink if you're getting these.] Sloane messaged Andy.

Andy started blinking.

"Sir?" Special Agent Thompson asked with concern. "Are you okay? Is something in your eye?"

Embarrassed, Andy stopped blinking.

[You're doing it aren't you?]

[Silly.]

[I can't actually see you.]

[Type something in so I know you're reading this now.]

[OK.] Andy typed.

[OK?]

[That's it?]

[At least it wasn't just K.]

[I hate when people just text K.]

[It's stupid.]

[Type okay. It takes like two seconds.]

"Mister Simmons," Special Agent Thompson said sternly. "You sure are on your phone an awful lot. May we ask who you're talking to?"

"Sorry. It's a client about her taxes. It's extremely confidential."

"Fine."

[They aren't really FBI.]

[What?] Andy messaged back.

"Sir," Special Agent Russell began. "It's imperative we find her and bring her in promptly."

[They're lying to you.]

[They're here to kill me.]

"Well, I don't know where she is. So, if there isn't anything else, I would like to spend the rest of the day with my daughter."

Special Agents Russell and Thompson stood up in unison and headed for the door. Andy opened it for them.

"If you get in contact with her, act naturally and give us a call." Special Agent Russell handed Andy his business card.

"If you see her, don't engage. She's considered extremely dangerous. Just call us, and we'll take care of the rest." Special Agent Thompson handed Andy his business card as well.

"If you see something, say something," Special Agent Russell said.

"Will do, gentlemen. But I'm entirely sure I'll never see this Sloane-woman again. In fact, she may even be halfway out of town by now. But if I do see something, I'll say something."

"Hey, Andy," Karen said, coming over to them carrying Samantha in her arms.

"Yes, Karen?" Andy returned, annoyed.

"I don't know what you and your girlfriend have planned for the rest of the day, but I need you to watch Samantha for me. I'll pick her up from your place later on, okay?"

"Girlfriend?" Special Agent Russell asked.

"Yeah, what girlfriend?" Special Agent Thompson asked.

"Slo–"

"She's not coming back for a while," he yelped, cutting Karen off. "I can, of course, watch and raise baby girl, Samantha," Andy said incoherently.

"Sir, are you having a stroke or something?" Special Agent Thompson asked. "Should we administer first-aid?"

"Yeah, are you okay?" Karen asked.

"Sure, I mean, go do what you have to, Karen. In fact, go do whatever it is you have to do right now."

"Fine. I'll be late."

"That's fine."

Karen put Samantha down and walked away while the child ran to her grandfather and Uncle Jerry.

Special Agents Russell and Thompson both looked at Andy with incredulous frowns.

"Well, I hope you gentlemen have a nice stay in Riders Bay. Happy hunting," Andy said.

Special Agents Russell and Thompson walked away, leaving the offices of Allied Accounting. As they left, they looked back at Andy over their shoulders with the same incredulous frowns.

Andy let out an enormous sigh of relief. A little bit of pee had come out during the end of his conversation with the special agents.

He wasn't sure who to believe.

On one hand, the agents seemed legitimate, and their report seemed to line up with what little he knew about Sloane. But on the other hand, Sloane was an exquisite beauty.

Andy received another text.

[Meet me at Jack Buck's place in an hour.]

[I'll need a ride back to the hotel.]

Andy didn't know what was going on. The intrigue to

follow Sloane was far too tempting. He walked to the conference room, knowing Frank and Jerry were there with Samantha. He would leave her with them. Not wanting to stay and explain himself to his father he only cracked open the door.

"Okay, honey, Daddy's got to go do something for the ridiculous blonde who's trying to ruin Daddy's life. I'll see you soon, okay, baby-girl?"

Samantha glanced up at her father and waved. Andy smiled and waved back.

He left before his father or Jerry could respond.

13

KAREN

Karen walked up the considerably long gravel driveway of the over two hundred-acre Rosenbaum estate. Though she was exhausted, and maybe a little tipsy, she was thankful this was the Rosenbaum's smallest estate out of the many they owned throughout the country. She inadvertently marveled at the stately, old-fashioned stone exterior, and the vines which grew along the high walls, careful not to walk on the impeccably kept, freshly mowed lawn. Oh, how she hated how much she loved the flowerbed, and quenched an overwhelming urge to stomp on the flowers. She even considered kicking over one of the decorative statues that lined the driveway, deciding against it due to its heavy size and the knowledge it would just end up being some other poor bastard's problem to fix.

Karen stood in the shadow of the massive Rosenbaum mansion. With thirty-five bedrooms, eight living room spaces, three large dining areas, two spacious breakfast nooks, twenty full bathrooms, fifteen half-bathrooms, and a kitchen large enough to run a major restaurant, the mansion was an incredible feat of luxury lifestyle.

And someone had to keep the toilets clean.

That's where Karen came in.

She hurried to the entrance for the work staff. Once inside, she made her way to the changing room where she found one of her co-workers.

"You're late," Debra said. She sniffed the air and squinted her eyes at Karen before going back to changing into her uniform. Karen pretended she didn't notice and joined her. The few sips shared with Sloane gave her a glow, but she was far from impaired.

Debra was a petite, Asian, twenty-something-year-old. She had pin-straight black hair and rosy cheeks. Her maid's uniform draped over her slender frame like a cloak.

"I know. I had to drop off Samantha. Where's Susan?"

"Later than you," Debra returned.

"How can that be? You two live together."

"She was out of the house before I left for work. I thought she'd be here."

"You know she hates working here."

"We all hate it. You hate it. But we got bills to pay, and I need her to do her part. We can't afford for her to get fired. We were late on another payment."

"I'm sorry to hear that."

Debra looked at Karen seriously. Karen braced herself for what came next.

"I know times are tough, but I was wondering–"

"I can't," Karen cut her off.

"It's only a couple hundred dollars. We can pay you back."

"No, you can't. I'm just as hard up as you are. I have a little girl to take care of. I'm sorry."

Karen closed the door to her locker after she finished

changing. She picked up a bucket of cleaning supplies and headed to do her rounds, starting with the twenty full bathrooms. Debra followed.

"What about Andy?" Debra asked.

"What about him?" Karen returned.

"Can't he help?"

"He's basically a child, too. I'm taking care of him more than Samantha. You should see him with his new girlfriend. He looks like a total dope next to her. She's completely out of his league."

"You were married to him."

Karen side-eyed Debra.

"Who is she?" Debra asked.

They were both on their hands and knees cleaning around a golden toilet which was hardly ever used.

"Who?" Karen asked.

"The girlfriend. Do I know her?" Debra asked.

"No. Some woman named Sloane."

"Oh, yeah. I know about her."

"How? She just got here."

"I was talking to Mary, and she brought her up."

"Mary from the hotel?" Karen asked.

"Yeah."

"You have to stop talking to Mary."

"Why?"

"You're going to make Susan jealous."

Karen and Debra moved from bathroom to bathroom, scrubbing the floors, tiles, shower heads, toilets, sinks, and light fixtures of wasted luxury.

"Do you think they'll stay together?" Debra asked.

"I give it another week, tops."

Debra and Karen dusted one of the many bedrooms when a bell rang. They knew exactly what it meant.

They stopped what they were doing and rushed downstairs.

The ringing persisted until they found its source in the east wing of the mansion. They walked quickly, careful not to break out into a jog. Karen and Debra dusted themselves and pressed down any creases in their uniforms as they rounded a corner, finding the source of the ringing.

"Yes, Missus Rosenbaum," Karen and Debra said in unison.

"Took you three long enough," Betsy Rosenbaum said without looking.

The Rosenbaum matriarch sat in the breakfast nook in the east wing of the mansion. She dined at a small, quaint table worth thousands of dollars. On the deceptively expensive table was a saucer with crumbs and a half-empty cup of coffee.

"Take this away, and help me bring my things to the sitting room."

Debra grabbed the saucer and cup while Karen struggled to find the possessions to which Betsy referred.

After a few moments of searching, Betsy glanced down, using her eyes to point out what Karen was supposed to help her with. On the opposite chair rested a newspaper from three days prior. The paper was folded in half twice and ripped near the top. Karen delicately picked up the newspaper and followed Betsy to the sitting room down the hall, rolling her eyes as she did.

Karen was used to Betsy's unusual orders. Whether it was to reheat a meal which was just served or to carry a newspaper thirty feet down the hall to another room, she had come to terms with her current situation. She needed the job, and the job was to do what she was told.

Once in the sitting room, Betsy rested at her usual end of the vintage couch. She held out her hand in complete silence, waiting for Karen to give her the newspaper until she finally cleared her throat to get Karen's attention.

"Sorry, Missus Rosenbaum," Karen said, handing Betsy the newspaper.

Thomas Rosenbaum walked into the room with some haste and over to the antique oval mirror hanging on the dark-blue papered wall. He fixed the collar on his blue-and-white checkered shirt so it stood above the lapels of this navy-blue sports coat. Pulling up his tan slacks, which rose above expensive brown leather loafers, he growled to himself in frustration that the slim brown leather belt barely held his pants and shirt against his protruding belly.

"Good afternoon, Mister Rosenbaum," Karen said.

Thomas barely noticed Karen on arrival and looked to see who greeted him. He responded in a gruff tone.

"Hello, young lady." He headed straight for the liquor cart. It was still the middle of the day, though she had no right to feel superior on that front, today of all days, and shifted her gaze to floor.

Debra returned with a fresh pot of tea and a clean cup, saucer, and teaspoon. She went to a nearby table to pour the tea for Betsy.

"Where's the other one?" Betsy asked.

"Who?" Karen replied after a moment, playing dumb.

"Stacey or whatever her name is?"

"Susan," Thomas interjected.

"Uh…" Karen looked over to Debra for help.

"I can't stay," Stanley, the younger Rosenbaum, said as he burst into the room.

"Why?" Betsy asked her son as he sat down on the vintage couch beside her. "Where are you going?"

"Over to Jack's place."

"Jack?"

"Jack Buck. Buck-O. Buckley. The Big-B. The Buckster. You know him."

Betsy shook her head in confusion at all the unnecessary nicknames.

"Anyway, he just called. Told me that Sloane-lady just showed up at his door."

"Sloane?" Thomas asked.

"That woman from last night at the Country Club. The one who left with that putz Simmons."

Clearly, Stanley was unaware the mother of Andy's child stood less than ten feet away from him.

"What's with that woman anyway? She seemed very odd," Betsy asked, readjusting the newspaper on her lap.

"What do you mean?" Stanley returned. "She was incredible. I'm going over there to meet with her. Jack told me she asked for me specifically."

"You hardly know this woman," Betsy said, concerned.

"I'm about to learn a whole lot more about her. Anyway, don't wait up. I'm having dinner at Jack's place."

"But I just prepared to have a private chef from Italy make us something."

"Sorry. Jack says he's got a sushi chef direct from Japan. And I've been craving some seafood."

He stood up, kissed his mother on the cheek, and headed for the exit.

As he left, he bumped into Susan, who rushed into the sitting room.

Susan had short blonde hair and was slender like Debra, but taller. She wore long-sleeves to cover up the full tattoos on both her arms. Betsy found them offensive and disturbing despite only being of roses and other various flowers.

"Sorry, sir," Susan said to Stanley as he rushed past her without a second thought.

"Where have you been?" Betsy asked, as Susan entered the sitting room.

"Sorry I'm late, Missus Rosenbaum."

"I don't pay you to be late. I pay you to be on time, promptly. And ready to do your assigned duties."

"Of course, Missus Rosenbaum. It won't happen again."

"Oh, I know that. You're fired."

Debra stopped stirring and dropped the spoon in the tea cup with a loud clank. Karen watched both Debra and Susan bow their heads in defeat as Susan gulped nervously.

"Missus–" Susan began.

"Good day," Betsy said, without looking Susan in the eye.

Deborah clasped her hands to her chest. "Please, Missus Rosenbaum. She didn't mean any harm by it. If you could just give her a second chance."

"No, no, no. No second chances. She's fired."

"Not fired," Thomas announced.

Thomas walked to the center of the sitting room, his brow lower than usual.

"Thomas," Betsy said in shock. "She is using us. Preying on our good will. She is stealing our time, and therefore, she is stealing our money."

"My money. And she stays. This young woman already has enough problems without us adding to them unnecessarily. We are a community, which means we provide services to one another. Susan, Debra, and Karen provide their maid-work, we provide the service of giving them a job in the first place. It's what makes our delicate society work."

Betsy turned away and grew silent. Thomas looked over to Susan.

"Thank you, Mister Rosenbaum," Susan said, gratefully. "It won't happen again."

Thomas moved over to Susan and stood by her side. He spoke lowly in her ear.

"It had better not. You have one chance more. Not another. I know you've fallen on hard times, and you are taking responsibility for your situation. No more lapses in focus from now on. Understand?"

Susan merely nodded, on the verge of tears.

"Now, don't you ladies have bedrooms that need tending to?" Thomas asked, addressing Debra and Karen.

"Yes, sir," Debra, Karen, and Susan said in unison.

Thomas nodded, and the three of them left the sitting room to head back upstairs and continue their other chores.

"What were you thinking?" Debra asked Susan.

"Leave me alone."

Karen, Debra, and Susan dusted the upper hall, working their way toward the closest suite.

"Where were you?" Debra asked.

"I said leave me alone."

"We can't afford for you to lose this job. You know how much we need this."

"I get it."

"Then tell me where you were."

"I went for a walk."

"For six hours?"

"I was thinking."

"What could you possibly be thinking about for six hours?"

"Do you really want to know what I was thinking about? Is it killing you not to know what's going through my head every waking second of every goddamned day? I was thinking to myself, 'why am I doing this? Why am I doing any of this?'"

"Doing what?"

"This. This stupid pointless job. Look at us. We're dusting a room that's never been lived in. This is all so meaningless. What's the point?"

"The point is we have bills to pay. Debts to pay. We owe people. I get it, we lost the bakery only five-years into getting it," Debra said, pulling Susan toward her by the hips.

"We were idiots to open that place right out of high school. And it was mostly your idea. So, what were you thinking?" Susan replied, tearing herself away.

She turned to the perfectly clean window and began wiping imaginary stains from it.

Debra wiped away tears as suddenly as they dropped from her lashes. She crossed her arms and turned her back to Susan. All the while, Karen scanned the two of them. Her eyes darted back and forth at the unfolding drama.

A part of Karen wanted to say something, to put their minds at ease; to remind them they were in this together and they only stressed themselves out further with this type of bickering. She wanted to tell them they had the same enemies, and the same goals.

Then she thought better of it.

It might have felt like the right thing to do in the moment, but not unlike when she refrained from kicking over a statue or stomping on the flower beds, it wasn't her responsibility to deal with any of this. She wasn't their marriage counselor. Their problems weren't her problems. But she would still have to listen to their arguments regardless.

"Why can't we just file for bankruptcy like normal people?" Susan finally blurted out as she turned from her pointless task.

"I'm not going to do that to my family," Debra said, her back still turned. "I'm not going to ruin my dad's life because of my choices. I told him we'd be able to pay the loan off in three years. That was six years ago. And we'll still need jobs, and we'll end up right back here anyway. At least this way we can open another shop in a few years."

"Are you fucking kidding me?" Susan asked throwing her hands in the air. "That's never going to happen. Hell, the Rosenbaum's won't even hire us as bakers. Did you know that, Karen?"

Karen nodded.

"He said he already has a baker from France, like that's supposed to mean something. That asshole said because we failed as a business then we must not be very good bakers. Face it, we had a dream. It came true for a while, then it died. Karen, you know what I'm talking about."

Karen tried to ignore their conversation and returned her focus on dusting around the windows that had never been opened.

"Do you want to know what I was thinking?" Susan asked. "I was thinking about how screwed up this town has become. There I was walking down Main Street, and all I saw was boarded-up business after boarded-up business. Roads with signs that fell to the ground, pot-holes, and faded lanes. I saw people who owned businesses for forty years going to their new jobs working as someone's servant. We're not the only ones, Debra. It's happening to everyone."

"What does that have to do with anything?" Debra asked. "So what if the streets are shit and places are out of business? We have debts that need to be paid, and I intend to pay them. I'm giving myself another chance down the line."

"Don't you get it? There is no second chance."

"Then tell me how it's the fault of people like the Rosenbaum's?"

"Other than the fact that we get paid just to get walked all over?"

"It's not their fault we've fallen on hard times. Things will get better."

"When?"

"Soon." Debra replied semi-confidently.

"That should have happened by now. The recession ended years ago. Other towns aren't having the same problems we're still having. Something's got to change," Susan told her.

"And what do you suggest, or is complaining all you're good for these days?"

"I have an idea," Karen said, moving away from her task.

Debra and Susan looked over at Karen.

"And that would be?" Debra asked coolly.

"It sounds to me like we need to invest in fixing up this town. If the place is reinvented, tourists will want to come back to Riders Bay, like before. And businesses will need to return – like before."

"How? And with what money?"

"With taxes."

"We already pay taxes."

"Yes, to the county, but not to the town. If we allocated funds to rebuilding the town, we can fix this place up in no time."

"The only way to do that is to raise taxes. No one can do that, and no one can afford it anyway."

"We elect a mayor. And maybe some other representatives. We're allowed to if we want. And we raise taxes, but only of the wealthier residents."

"That's not a bad idea, Karen," Susan said.

"It's a terrible idea. Who would even be the mayor?" Debra asked.

"I could do it," Karen suggested.

Debra scoffed at the suggestion.

"Don't scoff," Susan said. "It makes sense. Karen is one of us, she knows what we've all been through. She knows this town as well as anyone."

"But why her and not someone else? Someone more qualified," Debra asked.

"Why not me?" Karen asked.

"She's as qualified as anyone else I can think of. And she says she wants the job," Susan said. "So how do we get you elected?"

"Well, there just so happens to be a special fundraiser tomorrow night at the Country Club," Karen explained.

"During the last night of that stupid gala thing?"

"Exactly," Karen said. "Spread the word, ladies. We need as many people as possible at the Country Club tomorrow night. We got a town that needs fixing."

14

ANDY

Sloane had messaged Andy that she'd be at Jack Buck's place. Everyone in town knew exactly where the most famous person in Riders Bay lived. Even people who had never been to Riders Bay knew where he lived. His fame was monumental and had turned him into a tourist attraction. But, like the rest of the town's businesses, the pilgrimage just to see the outside of Jack Buck's home had slowed down significantly since he'd left the limelight and the flame that had been his fame faded.

The mansion was a post-modern architect's wet dream. Geometric shapes made up the exterior walls, painted an off brown with contours of dark grey.

Everyone in town utterly hated Jack's stupid-looking home.

Andy rang the doorbell. The chime had been replaced by the sound of a saxophone playing various jazz brass sounds.

He rolled his eyes. Even the doorbell was idiotic and pretentious.

A few moments later, Jack opened the door.

Andy's mouth suddenly got dry and it took him a moment before he said anything. He couldn't explain why he always got star struck around the guy, but as usual when he was in close proximity he choked on his words.

"Hi, Jack. Sorry to drop in announced. I—I 'm picking up a friend of mine," Andy stammered.

"No, no. We've been expecting you." Jack said eagerly.

Jack was tall and muscular. He'd kept his looks despite no longer desiring to be in movies. He'd made declarations in magazine interviews thirteen times before officially quitting the film industry.

Andy tried to stay as far behind Jack as he could, hoping to avoid the pungent overpowering scent of musky cologne wafting from the ex-famous movie star. No matter how far Andy was from Jack, though, the wreaking smell caught his nose. It wasn't until a few moments had passed that he realized the scent wasn't coming from Jack but the vents lining the intimately lit narrow hallway. Andy held back the overwhelming urge to gag.

Every time Jack turned around to check on his guest's progress, Andy was struck by his piercing deep blue-green eyes. Andy was dreadfully star-struck around Jack, despite not enjoying a single one of his blockbuster films.

Andy marveled at Jack's perfectly quaffed, dark brown hair. Maintaining some level of cynicism, he wondered if Jack's hair was even real. *Probably hair plugs.* Jack turned and smiled flashing his bright, pearly whites. *His smile is probably just as artificial as his stupid hair.*

Andy really didn't have anywhere else to look but at Jack as they wove their way through various halls and corridors which forced him to stare at the man's tight black t-shirt and blue skinny jeans. *The idiot probably paid three hundred bucks for the shirt, and a grand for the pants. I've got the same thing in a drawer at home that cost less than fifty bucks. Guess that's what you do when you got that kind of money.*

"This way. They're in the living room," Jack ushered.

Andy followed Jack through the entrance to a hallway on the right. The corridor snaked around until they were on the left side of the house. Andy rolled his eyes again. Fame aside, he still didn't much care for the man.

"This is such a fascinating feature," Jack said. "For every living space, you have to go right to go left, and left to go right. Truly ingenious."

"Yeah, a real genius came up with this," Andy said, sarcastically.

"Happy you think so. Anyway, tell me about Sloane."

"What do you want to know? I'm pretty sure I couldn't answer any of your questions."

"Is she always this *on*?"

"Absolutely."

"Fascinating."

"If you say so."

"She said you two have an arrangement."

"Why would she go and tell you that?"

"Well, I asked to sleep with her, before you arrived. She turned me down. I assumed the arrangement is a friends-with-benefits type of thing?"

"If she doesn't want to sleep with you, it's her decision and has nothing to do with me."

"I was only wondering if you two were exclusive. That's all."

"I met her yesterday, Jack. No, we're not exclusive. Whatever that means."

Andy had a pretty good idea what Jack was on about. He was a former movie star and wanted to know why he couldn't have now what he once could get so easily. Andy reveled in a sliver of joy knowing he had something over

Jack. It was petty, but he held onto it for a moment regardless.

"I thought you moved fast, Andy. Excuse me if I've offended you." Jack put both his hands together as if in prayer and bowed; a type of namaskar. "I've really gotten into Hindu spiritualism. I'm working on becoming more self-aware of my offensive comments."

"Thanks for sharing," Andy returned.

"You're very welcome."

Jack stopped, turned to Andy, and did another namaskar.

Andy didn't even bother controlling his eye roll as they resumed walking.

"Are we there yet?" Andy asked, annoyed.

"Yes, here we are." Jack waved his arm like a bull fighter...or magician.

A spacious but oddly furnished living room opened as if from nowhere. Much of the furniture sat pushed near the center of the room: a couch, two love seats, a recliner, a grand piano, three end tables, and a liquor cart.

Andy rubbed his forehead, giving himself a headache with the eye rolling.

Deep in the center of the stupid arrangement, Sloane closely nuzzled next to Stanley Rosenbaum. She giggled and whispered something into Stanley's ear. He laughed and touched and gripped her legs, which were crossed over his. She placed her arm around his neck, playing with his hair – then she noticed Andy and Jack.

That petty feeling of joy instantly turned into a petty feeling of jealousy. She played with some other fool's emotions, and Andy wasn't sure if he should just turn around and leave her there.

"Andrew, you finally made it," she said.

She uncrossed her legs from over Stanley's, stood up, and shimmied over to Andy.

Andy took Sloane by the hand. "Can I talk to you?" he asked.

"Weren't we just talking, Jack?" Sloane asked, ignoring Andy's request.

"Sloane, we need to talk." Andy wanted answers, and not just about what was going on here and why she needed him. He wanted to know why the FBI came to his office, and what she had to do with it.

"We *are* talking. Come, come, sit down."

Andy reluctantly followed Sloane back to the couch, squeezing his way through the ridiculous placement of the furniture. Jack followed.

"I love what you've done with this space," Sloane commented as they sat down. "It makes me feel claustrophobic, but in outer space."

"Thank you," Jack said.

Jack did another namaskar.

Stanley looked eagerly at Sloane. The younger Rosenbaum was tall and slender; not incredibly attractive, but with his confidence, one would assume he was a famous supermodel. He spent any chance he could with Jack, feeling his proximity to a superstar actor made him as much of a superstar. To Andy's annoyance, Stanley was also attracted to Sloane.

"Where were we?" Jack asked.

"Sloane was telling you about running for mayor," Stanley prompted, as he ran his hand through his dark hair, combing it back.

Andy was confused. "Mayor of what? I don't understand."

"Of Riders Bay, silly," Sloane replied. "He's usually much better at catching on to things."

"But Riders Bay hasn't had a mayor in decades."

"Of course not," Jack said. "And look where that's gotten this town. Sloane was just telling us this place is in shambles and businesses here are dropping like flies."

"You live here, she just arrived yesterday," Andy returned. "Why do you need a stranger to tell you how things work in a town you live in?"

"She's opened my eyes."

"Oh, your Buddhism didn't do that for you?"

"It's a process, and it's Hinduism."

"Whatever." Andy knew the difference, he just wanted to get under Jack's skin. As he suspected though, it seemed to have little effect on Jack's self-esteem.

"Andy, you are really being quite negative to a genuinely honest idea," Sloane said.

She gave Andy a look he was beginning to realize was the opposite of genuine. He didn't want to believe Sloane would lie to him about something so important. Her actions, though, made it difficult. If the FBI were real, then she lied just to get him to trust her. But he didn't trust her. He'd never had a chance to. Though he was completely transfixed by her, he realized more and more that her scheme was going too far. It was getting out of control and had implications which would affect all the residents of Riders Bay, not just a few of the rich ones.

Andy no longer believed Sloane was in any sort of mortal danger; the visit from the FBI agents was proof enough of that. She'd been anything but honest right from the start and had roped him into something he wasn't willing to participate in any longer.

"So, which of you is running for mayor again?" Andy asked.

"I am," Jack answered.

Andy threw his head back and laughed.

"I know it sounds outlandish. I mean, what would a person who hasn't been on a screen for nearly twenty years, and has never portrayed a true emotion except in a fictional setting, know about running a town? The answer is nothing," Jack said.

"And that's what makes it so perfect," Stanley interjected. "Who better than a complete outsider? Someone likable, someone completely approachable, someone people have been entertained by to run this town…"

"…into the ground," Andy finished.

"Andrew," Sloane said, sternly.

"No, Sloane. I have to object. This is stupid. What's your plan to fix the town's crumbling infrastructure? What's your plan to create jobs?"

"One word— gentrification," Stanley said. "My dad's been preaching it for years."

Andy put his face into his hands. "I don't care anymore. Do what you want. I just came to get Sloane."

"But wait. We didn't tell you the best part." Sloane said.

"We're going to hold a special fundraiser tomorrow night for Jack. On the last night of the gala," Stanley explained.

Sloane looked at Andy eagerly.

He nodded, still dejected. "Sounds like an idea."

"Splendid," Sloane said. "And your firm can handle all the money that will come in for Jack."

"Sounds great."

"Then, we can count on you?" Jack asked.

"On one condition," Andy said.

"Name it."

"You open the gala up to the entire town. No invitation required."

"What?" Sloane asked.

Andy registered the confusion in Sloane's voice. He didn't care. She played some sort of game; he just wasn't clever enough to figure out what yet. But, the confusion in her voice also meant she was caught off guard by his suggestion. She hadn't known he would call a bluff he didn't even understand. He'd get as many people as possible to see what she had in store for them.

"You heard me. Let the people in," Andy continued.

"They're going to be the ones possibly electing you. Let them hear your proposed plans. Let them all in on your master-platform that will save this town and transform their lives."

There was also another reason to bring everyone to hear Jack. Andy was sure no one would vote for such an idiotic, pointless, unqualified candidate as actor Jack Buck. The people of Riders Bay were smart. All they needed was to see what his dumb plan would be, and they'd laugh him off the stage.

"Let's not be hasty. He'll only have a single day to prepare. Let's keep this small-scale and private," Sloane said.

"No. He's right. I need to show the people I'm prepared to lead them. Stanley, get on the phone. We need to make some calls."

Stanley dialed a number on his smartphone. "Already on it."

"We'll see you tomorrow night," Andy said.

"Yes, yes. Tomorrow night," Jack replied, already on the phone himself.

Andy stood up, took Sloane by the hand, and squeezed them both past the moronic furniture to a hallway on the left. The corridor took them to the right, where Andy led Sloane through the front door and out of Jack Buck's post-modern excuse of a mansion.

15

SLOANE

Andy took Sloane by the hand and led her to his dull, tan, Japanese-made sedan. She nearly fell asleep just looking at it. Once inside the unremarkable car, the back of her thighs had the unfortunate displeasure of rubbing up against the scratchy beige interior. She winced in disgust at the unusual sensation. She shifted around in an attempt to get comfortable, which was futile in any car less than a hundred thousand dollars.

The entire time Andy drove through the sleepy streets of the town, Sloane wiggled about in her seat. They went over a poorly maintained road, passing the suburban area with houses of various sizes lining it. Magnificent mansions on massive properties sat sandwiched by tinier homes in disrepair.

Sloane looked out the window during short spurts of comfort. She noticed missing shingles on the roofs of the smaller homes, the chipped paint on the walls, the shattered windows, and the broken porches.

Then she observed beautifully manicured lawns, large flower beds, and the gravel driveways of mansions; the sporadic beauty of the massive properties versus the constant eye-sore of the homes surrounding them clearly showed the differences between the rich and the poor. She shrugged, bored. Sloane only looked out the window to distract herself from Andy's incessant complaining.

"You can't just go around doing whatever you want," he repeated.

He drove below the posted speed limit. It made her fidgety.

"This whole thing has gone on long enough," he said.

Andy drove so slowly, she was prepared to get out and walk.

"Do you hear me, Sloane?"

His whining made her teeth ache.

"I have a daughter to think about. A family to think about. My job to think about."

She was ready to hurl herself out of the car.

"I don't know what you're planning, but I don't want any further part of it."

She avoided eye contact, focusing on what she saw outside.

"Are you even listening?"

She turned to him, raised her eyebrows, and nodded in affirmation and he continued his tirade.

"The FBI came to my office today. Why were they looking for you? I had half a mind to tell them where you were."

She rolled her eyes.

"And how did you know they were there? Never mind. The point is you have not once been honest with me. And that's because you think only of yourself."

Andy was merely a scapegoat and nothing more. The

longer Sloane spent around him, the more aware he grew of that fact. It was probably why he'd interjected, making his suggestion to invite more witnesses to what she'd planned. What could he have possibly been thinking? She had to find a way to regain his trust and get him back on her side. He would still be useful, whether he like it or not.

Sloane reached in her purse to grab her phone. She'd have something planned to change his mind.

As she reached in her purse, though, she instead felt the cold, hard steel of her handgun. Something she always had with her. An occupational necessity. She couldn't go around waving it everywhere, but when worse came to worse, she'd be prepared.

Sloane considered taking it out, aiming it at Andy's head, and pulling the trigger. It would finally get him off her back. It would also put him out of his misery. He'd be out of the scheme for good. She could find someone else to serve in her plan: Jerry, Frank, Karen, Stanley, Jack – all of them were viable options. Any of them would eat out of the palm of her hand in a heartbeat.

Shooting Andy directly in the head, right then and there while he was driving, would normally be a danger to Sloane, but he was driving so slowly, she'd easily survive any potential accident.

She took a long, hard look at him as she gripped the handle of the handgun in her purse. It was then Sloane remembered why she chose him over the others at the Country Club. He was fearless. He was lovely. He was dim-wittingly charming.

She let go of the handgun and pulled out her phone. Slyly, she texted one of her contacts. Andy had to trust her for this to work.

He drove the car up to the valet at the Hotel Imperial. Sloane gave her hand to an attendant and left the car while

Andy dealt with the valet-driver. She kept walking as he tipped the man, gave him his keys, and took a ticket.

"Hey, I'm not done talking to you," Andy yelled after her. He ran to her side to continue his one-sided argument. "We're not finished yet."

Sloane silently walked over to the elevator and pressed the button, patiently listening to Andy's continued yapping. Occasionally, she nodded at what he said, not really registering any of it.

Andy crossed his arms as they entered the elevator. "Sloane, I'm done. No more."

Sloane nodded and made a noise in the affirmative. She pressed the button for the top floor, and as the elevator went up, she rummaged through her purse for her room key.

"You say they're not really FBI, but I can't take your word for it. Not anymore."

She nodded again and repeated the same affirmative noise.

"When your little scheme is done, whatever it is, I'm the one who's got to deal with the fallout."

She nodded again. He looked at her strangely and tilted his head. She'd made the wrong gesture. She instead puckered out her bottom lip, frowned, and started shaking her head.

"Yes, Sloane, it's true. I have a future to think about."

The elevator door opened, and Sloane walked out. Andy hurried after her. She rolled her eyes at his remark. He had no meaningful future, as far as she could see, and was as boring as he was gullible. Granted, his gullibility was one of the things she liked most about him, but it wasn't everything. He served a purpose, and she wasn't done with him yet. It was the only reason she kept the whining man-child around… wasn't it? Of course, it was.

When she reached the door of her Presidential Suite,

Sloane slid the room key into the slot, pushed the door open, and stopped dead in her tracks.

"No more games," Andy said, as he walked in beside her.

"He's right." A man standing in the middle of the suite turned to face them. "No more games."

He was a tall, well-dressed, striking man with a trim beard, dark skin, and a knowing smirk.

"Hola, Señorita Sloane," he said with a Spanish-accent.

Sloane knew exactly who this man was and why he was there. She cocked her head at the gun in his hand, replete with a silencer. Her eyes widened with shock. She hadn't expected him so soon.

"Shit," Sloane uttered.

16

ANDY

Sloane gasped, "Enrique, what are you doing here?"

"What do you think? I'm here to get what is mine."

"I don't know what you're talking about."

Andy also had no idea what the hell anyone was talking about. He was frozen in place, unable to move a muscle. Fear cemented his legs.

Enrique was armed.

He wore a black, dapper suit, had long, flowing black hair, and a beard. Looking as sophisticated as he did dangerous, he spoke in an elegant Spanish accent. It all absolutely intimidated Andy.

"I have nothing for you, Enrique," Sloane said, as she slammed the door to the hotel suite.

Andy gulped.

"Well then, you won't mind if I kill you both." Enrique raised the gun level to Sloane's head.

Andy gulped again. "Okay, okay," Andy said, raising his hands. "Can we just talk about this?"

"Excuse me, who the fuck are you?" Enrique asked.

"I'm Andy. Andy Simmons."

"Thank you for telling me your whole name. Now I will find your entire family and kill them all mercilessly."

Enrique pointed the gun at Andy.

Andy squealed, "Oh, my God. Please, don't kill anyone. You don't have to kill anyone. We can resolve all of this without resorting to violence."

"Are you sure about that?" Enrique asked.

"Yes, I'm sure."

Enrique lowered the gun.

For a moment, Andy saw a glimmer of hope. It made him smile. He had gotten through to the scary man with the gun, but wasn't out of the woods yet. If they talked long enough, Andy was sure they could reach some sort of agreement.

Andy could get money, if that was what Enrique was after. If it wasn't enough, he'd find a way to get more. They were going to work this out. Enrique was clearly a reasonable man; he'd proven it already by lowering his gun.

A shot rang out in the Presidential Suite. A bullet hit Enrique in his chest, directly at his heart, and he fell to the ground with a deafening thump.

Andy turned in a panic not understanding what was going on; not understanding who was shooting or why. He screamed a high-pitched squeal for an uncomfortable length of time.

Sloane moved over to Enrique's lifeless body, her gun steady over the corpse.

"He's dead, thank God," she said, in confirmation. "You can stop screaming now."

"What have you done?" Andy hyperventilated.

"I did what needed to be done. Thanks for the distraction, by the way."

"I wasn't trying to help you kill him. I was trying to reason with him."

Sloane feigned a smile and rested her hand on her heart. "That's so adorable."

"You're teasing me."

"No, no. That would have worked. You could have talked your way out of being murdered by a cold-blooded assassin. Sure."

Sloane bent over and picked up the body under the armpits.

"Come over here and help me. We have to move the body before–"

A knock at the door cut her off.

"We need to call the police," Andy said.

Sloane ignored him, dropped the body, and moved over to the door to check who was there.

"Aw, fuck," Sloane quietly mouthed.

She rushed back over to the body, resuming the disposal. Andy followed. He squeamishly picked up the ankles.

"We cannot trust the FBI," Sloane whispered.

They awkwardly moved the body to one of the bathrooms.

"Hurry up," Sloane whispered.

"Who's at the door?" Andy asked, as the knocking continued.

"I know you're in there," the voice on the other side of the door said. "I hear a man's voice. Who's in there?"

Sloane rolled her eyes.

"It's Enrique's man. His number one man," Sloane whispered. "And now he knows you're here."

"Me?" Andy said, this time as a whisper.

"That's right. And he won't be too pleased to see you've helped kill his boss."

"I didn't want to kill anyone."

This was out of control. Andy wanted out of this by any

means necessary. Sweat oozed from his pores turning his head into an oil painting of terror. Even his brain sweated as he tried to figure a way out of this crash of chaos. *Will I survive if I jump out of the window?*

They moved the body to the bathroom, then into the large shower, which Sloane stepped into as well.

"Go out there, distract him, the way you did earlier," Sloane said.

"That wasn't a distraction."

The knocking persisted.

"I swear to God, I'm going to have my boys break this fucking door down!" the voice on the other side of the door hollered.

"Listen, you have two choices. You can call the police and take your chances, hopefully the FBI aren't in cahoots with Enrique," Sloane offered. "Or you can just trust me, like you have so far."

"Why should I trust you?" Andy asked.

"Because I haven't held a gun to your head. Now go. You'll be fine. Just don't say anything that'll get you killed."

She pushed him out of the bathroom and shut the door. He heard the click of the lock.

Andy gulped once more.

The knocking turned into slamming as Andy approached the door. He passed by a table with a hotel phone on it. It would only take a few seconds to call the police and tell them where he was and what just transpired. He could confess his involvement and hope for the best. Andy was sure he could afford a pretty good attorney with the money he no longer had to offer Enrique. Maybe he would only have to spend about a decade in prison with good behavior. He could still get out with enough time to see his daughter graduate from high school. That was, unless the trauma of having a criminal father turned her into a dropout and she was forced to get into pornography to make ends meet.

The slamming shook Andy out of his hesitance. As he turned the handle, the door burst open, and three men rushed forward into the suite.

"Hi, can I help you fellows?" Andy asked, nervously.

"Sit him down," the smaller man told the larger two.

The big guys forced Andy to sit on the couch. They stood on either side of him like pillars of terror. The smaller man sat down across from him. Andy shook noticeably as the small man flashed a sinister smile.

"Hello. You can call me Jackson. This is Juan, and this is Carl." Jackson gestured to his associates as he named them.

"I'm Carl, he's Juan," the large man standing over Andy's right side said, correcting his boss.

"Whatever."

"I'm just getting things straight," Carl said.

Andy knew what the men were capable of by the sheer terror they instilled in Sloane. He certainly didn't want to be anywhere near men she thought were dangerous.

"Listen, I don't know what to tell you. I don't know anything," Andy said.

"Don't worry about it. That's what we're here to find out. Get his wallet," Jackson said.

Juan violently grabbed Andy, pulling him up. He checked the inside of Andy's jacket, then the back pocket of his pants until he found the worn-down, brown, leather wallet. Juan handed it to Jackson and violently thrust Andy back down onto the couch.

"Seriously, guys. I don't know–" Andy began again.

"You don't even know what I'm here to ask you. For all you know, I'm here to ask about my taxes," Jackson said as he pulled out Andy's driver's license and one of his Allied Accounting business cards.

"Okay, sure, fine. Let's talk about your taxes," Andy said.

Jackson slipped the license back into the wallet, pocketed the business card, and flung the wallet at Andy who awkwardly caught it and looked up to the vindictive stare of the man sitting across from him. Jackson pulled out a revolver. Andy pissed himself.

"Do I look like I want to talk about my mother-fucking taxes?" Jackson asked, menacingly.

Andy sweated. He gulped, trying to return moisture to the barren, desert-like wasteland of his mouth, and quickly rethought every decision which brought him to that moment; what he felt would be one of the last moments of his life. Some woman would be the reason he was going to die.

"This is a revolver," Jackson said, about the source of Andy's impending death.

Andy nodded knowingly, then quickly shook his head in confusion.

"You understand?" Jackson said.

Of course Andy knew what a revolver was. What he didn't understand was why it would be needed.

"You don't–" Andy again was cut off.

"There are six cylinders in this pistol," Jackson said.

Jackson pulled out a single bullet from his coat pocket. He opened the cylinder, slipped the bullet inside, and spun it. With a quick flick of his wrist, the chamber shut, and the spinning stopped. The location of the bullet remained unknown.

Jackson smiled as he looked at Andy.

"Andy. Can I call you Andy? Well, I'm going to call you Andy instead of scared-little-white-boy. I'm sure you're familiar with a game called Russian Roulette."

Andy nodded and gulped again. He knew what was coming. More importantly, he knew his odds of survival.

"I'm just an accountant," he whimpered.

"Sure, you are. What I'm going to do is point this gun at your head. If you don't answer my questions, I pull the trigger." Jackson aimed the weapon at Andy's head. "Do you understand?"

Andy stuttered. Of course he understood. All too well.

"I don't know any–"

Click.

Andy flinched and closed his eyes at what he'd expected to be the end of his life. The click he heard, as well as the snickering from the two giants on either side of him, was indication enough that he hadn't died, just yet.

"Where's Sloane?" Jackson asked.

"I don't–"

Jackson pulled the trigger again.

Click.

Another empty cylinder represented another chance lost for Andy's attempts to solve this problem with diplomacy. Jackson was a tough guy. Andy needed to match the homicidal toughness with his own suicidal robustness.

"Where's Sloane?" Jackson asked again.

"You really want to know where she is?" All the nervousness turned into adrenaline.

Click.

"She's downstairs."

Click.

"Or maybe she's in here."

Click.

"All I know is I'm not going to tell you a word. I'm not going to do that to her. I'm not going to hand her over to a bunch of thugs."

Jackson smiled and pulled the trigger again.

Click.

Jackson, Juan, and Carl all laughed hysterically. They laughed for an uncomfortable amount of time. After a while, Andy laughed as well.

"You got spunk, guy," Jackson said, wiping away tears. "I wasn't about to kill you. If you'd sold out Sloane, I would have had my boys here rip your balls off and shove them down your throat, then I would have killed you. We only kill snitches."

Andy let out a stuttering sigh of relief. He began crying. He was going to live.

"If you see Sloane, will you tell her Jackson's been looking for her? That would be a great help. Thanks."

Jackson stood up and made his way to the door, with Juan and Carl following. They left Andy alone in the hotel suite. He was too afraid to stand. A puddle had formed just under him.

HOURS LATER, Andy and Sloane shuffled along the pier, throwing Enrique's dead body into the harbor. He was still in shock, not even certain how they'd gotten there. The entire ordeal had gone beyond too far.

"What the fuck!" Andy yelled, finally breaking his silence.

Sloane shushed him.

"Don't silence me, woman. I was almost killed twice in an hour."

"You're being dramatic," Sloane said.

"I can't do this. I tried, but I can't keep doing this."

"Who cares about you?"

"What?"

"Was that you back there saving yourself?"

"Yes."

"No. You were protecting me."

"You put me in the middle of this."

"Yes, but you chose to trust me. You chose not to tell Jackson where I was." A hitch in her voice betrayed her emotions. "You protected me. You have trusted me, and you have prospered because of it."

"Prospered? Are you out of your goddamned mind? Might I remind you, I was almost killed. Twice!"

"Please, do stop reminding me. You were muttering that the whole way here in the car."

"I was? I don't remember."

"Honey." Sloane moved over to Andy and put her hands on either side of his waist. She pulled him in close until they were chest to chest. She looked directly into his eyes.

If Andy wasn't so mesmerized by her striking emerald gaze he would have looked away. He was complicit in a murder and the disposal of a body. Whatever there was left of his life, it was over, and he knew it.

"In all my travels, no one has ever done what you've done for me." Sloane continued.

"I wonder why?" Andy asked, sarcastically. His smirk quickly faded. He wasn't really joking. Not about this. His feelings toward her had morphed from fondness and affection, to fear and mistrust. Now, he feared they would morph again into something far worse… far deeper.

"We're almost done. Just one more day, and we'll be home free," she told him.

"That's just it, Sloane. I don't want even one more day."

Sloane looked away. Andy knew he'd stung her. He almost cared that he'd hurt her.

"Then it seems you have another choice to make," Sloane said, returning her emerald gaze back to him. "Continue to trust me, or put your faith in those who have threatened and intimidated you. Choose wisely."

Sloane pressed her lips to Andy's. She closed her eyes and held him tightly. Her fingers gripped the sides of his arms as she pressed her chest harder into his.

His eyes remained open, looking down at her wondering if his fear and mistrust had finally transformed into utter disgust.

17

JERRY

Jerry was incapable of knowing when to stop when he was doing too much. He was equally incapable of catching onto what others seemed to grasp just fine. That day, the Jonas's sat across from Jerry at his long, glass desk, in the largest office in the building.

Jerry contemplated the size of his office in comparison to Andy's, wondering if he truly earned it. As he sat in silent scrutiny, he also waited for someone to say something.

The office was meticulously and rather profusely decorated with model airplanes of all types – jet-fighters, commercial, G5s, old World War II-era planes of all sorts, as well as older World War I-era planes – accented the room. He didn't have a particular interest in planes, though. Jerry had seen a catalogue picture of an office decorated the same way. He'd thought it was a neat idea for his own office and went overboard collecting items to scatter around.

Jerry's gaze wandered back to Walter Jonas who wore a

bespoke suit with a bowtie, a vest, and a tweed jacket. His much more accomplished wife, Abagail Jonas, wore a simple black dress with a black scarf. She kept looking over her shoulder, checking to make sure her large mink coat hadn't fallen off the hanger again. Then she looked out the window. The weather in Riders Bay grew worse.

"What is it with this ungodly unseasonable weather this morning?" Abagail asked, musing aloud.

"No one knows when it will end," Walter said.

Walter and Abagail were going over their finances for the third time that year. They'd put together and filed their taxes to see if there was anything left in their accounts to expand upon their estate. However, they already knew they didn't have the money. Yet, they wanted to maintain the illusion they still had a vast wealth from which they could continue to draw.

Jerry kept silent as he went over the stack of documents he'd printed out for them. The silence lasted for a half an hour. He rattled his fingers on the desk for a time, before Walter reached out and rested his hand on them. Jerry stopped and looked up.

"You know a great many things happened during the eighth century," Walter began, attempting to break the awkward silence.

Jerry looked up, confused. "Like what?" he asked.

"Well, for instance, just off the top of my head, in year 705, Empress Wu Zetian was overthrown," Walter said.

"Okay?"

"She was China's first and only Empress."

"Oh."

"And it is also the estimated century *Beowulf* was written."

"Beo-who?"

"*Beowulf*. One of the premier English epics."

"I didn't know that."

Jerry looked back down at the files he thumbed through.

He wasn't someone who had any interest in history. Most of it, to him, was painfully boring, pointless nonsense which had no impact on him whatsoever.

Walter rolled his eyes at Jerry's ineptitude. Jerry had heard he was fascinated with the eighth century, feeling it was one of the most essential periods in all of human history. By contrast, Jerry was bored to exhaustion every time he was subjected to one of Walter's pedantic lectures.

"Did you know Johann Sebastian truly enriched already established German styles through his skill in counterpoint, harmonic, and motivic organization?" Abigail said, trying her own attempt at breaking the bedrock-hard silence.

"Yo-who?" Jerry asked. "Is he one of Beo-guy's friends?"

"Johann Sebastian Bach. I play so much Bach. I've read so much of his sheet music I feel I know him personally. I always refer to him as Johann Sebastian."

"Is he a friend of yours from school or something?"

"He's been dead for over two hundred years."

"That's a weird kind of friendship."

"He was a composer… of music."

"Like classical music?"

"During the Baroque period."

"Is that when women dance in their underwear?"

"No, that's burlesque, not Baroque."

Abagail retreated back into silence, utterly offended by Jerry's lack of knowledge in music.

"Well, I see here–" Jerry began, as he looked back down at the files.

Stanley Rosenbaum cut him off as he burst into the office. Startled, Jerry threw the forms up in the air and hovered over his seat a full two feet.

"There you are," Stanley said as he bogarted his way into Jerry's office.

"Stanley, what are you doing here?" Jerry asked coming

back down to his chair, frantically gathering and reorganizing the forms as his heart rate returned to normal.

"I'm in special need of your special services."

Jerry hovered again in his chair. A wide smile appeared. Overjoyed, he ignored the clients he already had sitting in front of him.

"Yes, sir," Jerry said.

He stood up and took Stanley by the arm, leading him farther into the office and giving him his chair. Stanley leaned back immediately, combing his hair, and resting his feet on Jerry's desk. Jerry was still overjoyed as he hovered nearby, putting his back to Walter and Abagail.

"What do you need from me, sir?" Jerry asked, his hands clasped in front, his head in a slight bow.

"Cut the sir shit, Jerry."

"Yes, sir."

"I need you and this firm to watch the finances for the gala tonight."

"What do you mean?"

"We're holding a fundraiser and I need you guys to set up some sort of account or whatever it is you people do."

"You don't need us to handle your taxes?"

"What taxes?" Stanley replied with a smug smile.

Jerry was suddenly extremely disappointed. His clasped hands fell apart, and his shoulders slumped down. Just as soon as he had caught a big fish, it slipped from his grasp.

"Is this a problem or something?" Stanley asked, noticing Jerry's disappointment.

"I don't know if that's something we can do for you," Jerry said, filled with melancholy.

"You guys are accountants, aren't you?" Stanley asked as he stood up, trying to gain composure over Jerry.

"Well, yes—"

"Good. I have a job for you guys to account for all the

money coming in tonight. Don't worry. Your firm will be compensated."

"It's not that."

"Then what is it?"

Jerry wanted business. He was in a position of some authority with Allied Accounting, and made it his personal responsibility to drum up more high-end clientele for his firm. For as long as he had been in his position as senior partner, the only new clients he could bring in were the Jonas's.

"I don't think we'll have the time to set up the necessary systems," Jerry finally said in defeat.

"Why not?" Stanley asked growing frustrated. "I'm not going to let Jack down on this one, so you had better get your shit together. Didn't Andy fill you in about this already?"

"No, and he shouldn't have signed off on anything without my approval."

"Why does he need your approval? Doesn't he run this place?"

This struck a nerve in Jerry he didn't think he had in him to strike. He wasn't a proud man, or an assertive man, or even just a manly-man, but he was a professional. Too much time and hard work had gone in for Jerry to just be relegated to an afterthought.

"Let me tell you something, buster." Jerry's chest rose, and he stood up straight.

It was the first time he actually stood at his full six-foot-four-inch height since the last time he was forced to, on his most recent doctor's visit. Stanley's eyes widened in astonishment.

"I'm the senior partner of this firm, not Andy. So, if you want our services you come to me and place a request. No one goes over my head." Jerry stuck his finger into Stanley's chest.

"Fine," Stanley submitted. "It's just that the rate is ten percent of whatever we bring in."

As much as Jerry loved that he was finally showing some backbone, he loved the idea of getting his firm ten percent of what would be millions of dollars in donations even more. Sure, it was a little underhanded, but business was business and no one would be checking their books anyway.

"Plus, there will be a hell of a lot of potential clients there," Stanley said.

Jerry wanted to maintain his domineering demeanor, but found it increasingly difficult as he got giddier. Everything he wanted finally fell into his lap: the chance to pull in clients, and gaining the firm more revenue upfront. Jerry was going to give in, but he also wanted to keep the feeling of command.

"That sounds great!" Jerry barked angrily, his grateful words not at all matching his gruff tone.

"So, you'll get everything set up?" Stanley asked, a little confused.

"Yes, we'll get right on it, goddamnit!"

"What about us?" Walter asked. "I thought we still had business to discuss."

"I'm sorry." Jerry turned to face his clients and softened his tone. "You two are terribly short on funds."

"Well, what should we do?" Abagail asked.

Jerry took a moment to consider the question. Then he turned back to Stanley, his frown returning.

"I'll need you to give Abagail a gig for tonight," Jerry barked at Stanley. "My clients would appreciate the opportunity."

"All right, fine. She can play her stupid Classical music during the gala."

"Actually, it's burlesque—"

"Baroque," Abagail corrected.

"Excuse me, Baroque, and it's not stupid! Now, if you

don't mind, I have further business to discuss with my clients. I'll come to you later with the details."

Stanley put his hands up in further submission, and backed away slowly before turning around to head for the door. His eyes were wide with confused astonishment as he left Jerry alone with Abagail and Walter.

"I'm loving this firm more and more, Walter," Abagail said, very pleased.

"I know. We only came in here to see if we had the money to get that extension for our heated indoor Olympic-sized pool, and instead we're leaving here with more money," Walter said with an air of superior satisfaction.

"Oh, you still won't have the funds necessary for that extension," Jerry interjected as he returned to his seat.

Abagail and Walter simply looked at Jerry as though he'd just accused them of murder. Without another word, Jerry looked back down at his clients' forms, the awkward silence more deafening than before.

18

ANDY

"This woman is going to be the death of me," Andy said, as he stood in the conference room with Jerry and his father the morning after his ordeal.

Andy's hair was unkempt. One of his pant legs pinched in his black crew sock, and while his shirt was freshly ironed, it smelled of mildew and was only half-tucked in. He treaded around the conference room with an air of authority and the look of a neurotic. His body occupied the room, but his mind was still trapped in Sloane's Presidential Suite.

"Son," Frank said, standing in front of him to stop the erratic pacing. "She can't be all that bad."

Frank placed his hands on either side of Andy's shoulders, a gesture of reassurance. Andy, in turn, merely crossed his arms, avoiding his father's gaze. He shook away from Frank's embrace, then continued pacing.

"She is, trust me," he said, gravely.

"Well, tell me what happened." Frank followed Andy through the room.

"I really can't."

"Why not?"

"Some of it you wouldn't believe. Hell, I don't even believe half of what that woman has told me."

Andy wasn't sure implicating his father in the sordid affairs of Sloane's would be the correct way to go. He badly wanted some advice, but couldn't possibly expect to get any good suggestions if he merely provided half the information. It only stressed him out further contemplating his options.

"I believe in her. And I believe in you," Frank said, still with a tone of reassurance.

"What does that have to do with anything?" Andy frowned.

"I'm just being supportive."

"You want to support me? Then tell me how to break up with Sloane."

"I can't do that."

"Why?"

"Because I think she's great for you. She's beautiful, smart–"

"Dangerous."

"Dangerous? No, she can't be."

"She is. She's deadly."

Andy wanted to tell his father in that very moment everything of which Sloane was capable. He hesitated, and hoped Frank didn't notice his sudden apprehension.

"Granted, she has a strange name," Frank remarked, mostly to himself. "I still don't know what kind of name Sloane is."

"It's a normal name, Dad. We've been over this already." Andy ran his hands over his face and shook his head as he sat in one of the office chairs.

Frank settled next to his son. "Okay, but dangerous? She's a nice lady."

"Why would you think that?"

"Because I met her, and she seems nice."

"She seems like whatever she wants you to think she seems like."

"What?" Frank frowned trying to follow his son's incoherent sentence.

"You know what I mean. Just trust me, and stop trusting her."

Frank threw his hands toward Andy. "Oh, come on."

"I need to stay away from her."

"You need her."

"Why would you say such a thing? Haven't you been listening?"

"You really do need her."

"I can't believe I'm hearing this."

"She isn't a threat to you, is she?"

"Yes, she is."

"How?"

"She puts me in bad situations. Uncomfortable situations."

"You mean she gives you a sense of adventure. A sensation, maybe, you've never felt before. She's taking you out of your comfort zone. What's the matter with that?"

"Dad, she's great. There are times I look at her and think she's the most beautiful woman in the world. And if my final moments are looking at her, I could die a worse death than that."

"Now, tell me how it's supposed to be bad for you to think that way about a woman you love."

"Love? Dad, don't be ridiculous. I haven't even known her long enough to–"

"Are you sure?"

"But Karen…" For the first time Andy got a question only he

had the possibility of answering, and he was strangely on the verge of saying he was in love with her. Sloane, in a very limited way, had taken Andy on an adventure, one of which he would not soon forget. But was it love? Andy couldn't say for certain.

"I don't know," he rested his head on the desk.

"I was married to your mother for thirty-five years before she died. And how you feel about Sloane is how I felt for your mother every single day. I don't even remember you ever talking about Karen this way."

"It was different with Karen."

"Exactly, and that's why it never worked between you two. The only good thing to come out of that marriage was Samantha."

"By the way, speaking of Samantha, can you watch her tonight? I'm going to the stupid gala thing."

"No problem. Going with Sloane?"

"Actually, it's Karen. She's doing something at the gala. A speech, I think."

"A speech about what?"

"Not sure. I didn't ask. Whatever it is, she seemed excited about it when she called me last night."

"And what about Sloane?"

"What about her?"

"Are you going with her?"

"Yeah. I should be headed for the airfield on the other side of town and hopping on a chartered flight out of the country. Instead, I'll probably be seeing her there."

"You need her."

"Stop saying that." Irritated by his father's persistence, Andy stood up from his chair and paced away. He needed more time to consider this; instead, Frank pressed the issue Andy wasn't at all ready to address.

"You don't have a lot of things going on in your life," his father said.

"And whose fault is that?" Andy asked, gesturing to his dad as he spun on his heels.

"What are you talking about? How is that my fault?"

"You made Jerry a senior partner and the executive vice president of the firm."

"So?"

"I'm your goddamned son, for Christ's sake." Andy leaned in closely toward Frank, eyes wide with contempt.

"So?"

"Dad, it's customary to make your child the second in charge of your company."

"Why would I do that?"

"I just told you!"

"Andy, let me explain something to you. I didn't make you the executive vice president of the firm because you haven't earned it yet. To you, this is just another job, like any other. And I know why you became an accountant. You did it because I'm an accountant, and you didn't know what else to do with your life. Why would I thrust a position onto you that you don't really want? Why would I force you to do anything you didn't want to do? This isn't just a job for me. This is my life. It always has been."

Andy lowered his head and shoved his hands in his pockets. He'd taken a job at his father's firm out of a sense of obligation. He hadn't considered why his father was giving him an opportunity like this in the first place.

"I didn't know. I don't mean to disappoint you, Dad. You've given me everything in my life because of this firm."

"I know, and I want you to feel as though you've earned what I leave behind for you. You don't disappoint me, son. You never will." Frank stood up, moved over to Andy, and rested his hand on his shoulder.

"Thanks, Dad."

"I didn't want to spring this on you at the last minute, but now seems as good a time as any to tell you." Frank turned, returned to his seat, and bowed his head down.

"Tell me what?"

"It's in my will that you take over the firm, if that's what you want, in the event of my death."

"Your will?"

"I've been keeping up with it lately. Just in case something untimely were to happen to me."

"Nothing untimely is going to happen to you, Dad."

"Well…"

"You aren't dying."

"Well…"

"Dad!"

Frank grew silent.

The silence hung in the room. Andy's heart sunk as he contemplated all the things he regretted in his life; all the gifts his father had imparted that he only turned to squander.

"Dad?" Andy asked softly as his eyes welled up.

"You know how I've been away a fair bit lately? Well, that's because I've been seeing some doctors."

"Doctors?"

"Specialists."

"What the hell, Dad? When were you going to tell me?"

"I didn't want to alarm you if there wasn't anything to report."

"Did they find anything? Is there something wrong with you? Are you okay?" Andy placed a hand on his father's.

"It's okay. It might be nothing." Frank waved away his son's hand.

"Which is it? Is it nothing, or is it something?"

"I don't know yet. It just put everything into perspective for me. If I'm going soon, I want to make sure my boy has everything he needs to take care of his girl."

"Dad, I'll be fine."

"Besides, Jerry really needed his position. Becoming the

executive vice president of the firm might have been the single best thing that ever happened in his life."

"Yeah."

Andy and Frank nodded in agreement. Then they turned, having forgotten Jerry was still sitting in the conference room. They awkwardly smiled at him. He smiled back, unfazed.

"You guys keep going," Jerry said with a tear in his eye. "I love when you two open up like this. It's so heartwarming."

19

KAREN

The early evening air hung damp and hushed. Except for the murmurs of the people milling toward the Country Club, it remained silent. A quiet before an inevitable storm. Around the corner of the stage, the area near the back entrance of the dining hall served as a behind-the-scenes. From there, Karen could see everyone in attendance.

The dining hall of the Country Club was packed to capacity. The dimly lit hall breathed as the sunlight peering through the old wooden shudders died out. Soon, the only light would come from the faulty florescent lamps on the vaulted ceiling.

The crowd gathered in front of the makeshift stage ordinarily used by the DJ. Abagail Jonas played her violin along with three other violinists to form an impromptu quartet. The DJ was gone, not even invited to the last day of the gala, much to Abagail's delight, as far as Karen could tell.

More people than Karen expected milled about with

whispered conversations. It terrified her. She shook as she shuffled through her index cards full of talking points, clever witticisms, and words of encouragement she'd written for herself a few hours before the gala.

Scanning the sea of people she would soon address, she noticed residents she'd known since childhood: plumbers, electricians, carpenters, and other current and former small business owners. Susan and Debra stood toward the front of the stage. They caught her eye and waved with eager encouragement.

Karen wanted to throw up.

She looked over to her right where Jack Buck prepared to speak. Having had no idea she'd be running opposite a famous movie star, she clutched her stomach with one hand and used the other to steady herself with the wall, smashing her index cards in her grip. Her eyes squeezed shut as she tried to breathe slowly, but had difficulty concentrating over Jack's vocal exercises.

A firm hand grabbed her shoulder and swiftly turned her around, nearly causing her to lose the contents of her stomach. She opened her eyes and found Stanley Rosenbaum standing in front of her.

"What the hell are you doing here?" He asked.

"What do you mean? I'm going to speak."

"About what? Proper dusting habits?"

"No, I'm running for mayor."

Stanley smiled, barely containing his amusement. When he realized Karen wasn't joking his smile disappeared.

"You're running for mayor?" Stanley asked.

"Yes." Karen gulped. She hadn't really processed what her opposition would be like. And now that she faced it, she became even more ill to the verge of collapse. A chill of intimidation ran up her spine, and she wasn't sure how to handle it.

"Against Jack? You're running against Jack?"

"If he's running, too, then yes."

"And you thought you'd use tonight, the gala we're holding and financing, to campaign?"

Karen stuttered out a short response that came as little more than a chirp.

"Yeah, you're going," Stanley ordered, pushing her towards the door.

"No," Karen said, firmly. "I'm not going until I have said what I've come here to say."

"Hello, my darlings." The British accent was distinctive.

"Yes, Sloane?" Stanley asked, as he turned to greet the woman.

Stanley's demeanor completely changed from annoyed to jovial.

"What seems to be the problem?" Sloane asked.

"Oh, nothing. I'm handling it," Stanley said, as he continued to push Karen from the backstage area.

"He won't let me speak," Karen said, holding herself back using the doorway to brace herself.

"Ah, I see. Well, I'm afraid I'm going to have to agree with Stanley. This is a fundraising engagement, not an open forum for debate."

"What about all that stuff you were telling me about taking back power?" Karen asked.

"That was strictly lady talk. You were being a whiney little twat. I had to say something to shut you up."

"She's not a whinny little twat," Andy said, as he walked from the backstage toward them.

"What the hell are you doing here?" Stanley asked.

"I'm handling the money coming in tonight, remember? Jerry and I are set up back here," Andy said.

"Well, honey, I don't know how much you know–"

"Karen's running for mayor. Sounds like a good idea," Andy interjected.

"Excuse me?" Sloane's head spun around before the rest of her body as she squared up to Andy.

"Why the hell are all these people here if not to hear from the candidates?" Andy asked directly into Sloane's face, their noses less than an inch apart. Something sparked between them and it scared Karen.

"They're here so they can each give me – us, I mean, us – their donations to have a free, open, and fair election," Sloane said.

"Free, open, fair. Sounds good. Then Karen should speak."

"Andy's right," Jack said, as he approached the group. "How can the people appreciate all I'll do for them unless I run against someone?"

"Well, I wouldn't put it that way–"

"I'll debate you, Kerry."

"It's Karen."

"Right. We'll do this for the people."

Jack bowed and went back to the corner, continuing his vocal exercises.

Andy nodded. "It's settled, strangely. The debate is on."

"Fine." Sloane stormed off.

Karen noticed a look between Sloane and Andy. A look between two people who shared a secret; a combination of fear and rage. The look that warned the other person of what would come of their fate if ever the secret were revealed. Karen shook it off. It was none of her business and she really didn't have any time to dwell on it anyway.

Stanley let go of Karen, shot both her and Andy dirty looks, and followed Sloane.

"I didn't need your help," Karen said.

"Didn't look that way to me." Andy chuckled.

"I'm serious. I'm serious about all of this. I always run away when things get hard for me. I can't run away again."

"What are you talking about?"

Andy was attentive. Something had changed in him. He

wasn't being confrontational or dismissive. He showed something Karen hadn't seen in years: compassion.

Karen would no longer act meek or indecisive. She stood surefooted and purposeful. In that moment she realized Andy had never seen her do something special. They had met after her business failed. She only ever was a mother and an ex-wife to him, not someone looking forward to the future.

"Us, for starters. Things got hard, and I ran away from you. And now all I can think about every night is you."

Andy didn't respond.

"I was so fucking stupid," Karen said, throwing her head back as she leaned against the doorway. "I was afraid of things changing."

Andy kept silent.

"I thought I was jealous because you're my ex and the father of my child. But I don't know how to be with anyone else because I never have been. I guess I was insecure about you being with Sloane because it's different, and I don't know what to do with different. But I'm not afraid anymore. I have something I want, something I'm going to fight for. I'm not running anymore. So, you go do what you want. And I'll do what I want."

Andy nodded in approval.

"Now go," Karen said. "I have to prepare."

"Good luck," Andy said, as he stepped away. "But you won't need it."

20

ANDY

"How much is there so far?" Sloane asked, eagerly.

She stood just behind and to the side of Jerry, looking over his shoulder while he sat reading a spreadsheet on a laptop. Andy came in through the backstage area, more than twenty feet away from the two who sat at a table by the back exit. Andy watched Sloane's every move and expression.

The end of the backstage area was dark. A low desk lamp and the blue beam from the laptop were the only sources of light. It cast Sloane in shadow, accentuating the devious look on her face.

"Well, we've got about twenty grand alone from the entry fees," Jerry replied.

Sloane's eyes widened with glee.

"Yes, yes, go on." She nearly squealed with joy.

"We've already gotten over three million in donations for Jack. And another two grand for Karen. I didn't know she was running for mayor. Good for her," Jerry said.

"Who cares? Where's the rest of it?"

"Oh yeah, there was another eighty grand from the silent auction. What exactly are we auctioning off again?"

"Don't worry about that now. How's the money being processed? Cash? Check?"

"Well, everyone paid electronically, so it went into the account for the election. Here it is."

Sloane looked closer at the screen showing the various account numbers of the donors. Andy walked up behind her as she gave in and squealed cheerfully. She clapped her hands and hopped in place.

"What are you so happy about?" Andy asked as he slowly approached.

The music started; Sloane turned her head in search of the tune.

"Ah, 'Por Una Cabeza,'" she said in revelation.

Sloane took Andy's hand and led him to the dance floor. The area cleared away as they stepped forward. The wind outside the Country Club picked up. The rain thrashed hard now. The sound of the tango the quartet played warred with the thunderous weather outside.

It was clear to Andy that Sloane didn't care; that much was certain as she threw her head back with laughter. It was all music to her: The rain, the quartet, her devious cackling at how smoothly her plan worked out.

Andy led the tango, moving them about the dance floor with effortless grace. He kept his posture straight, and his grasp on Sloane firm. This was more than a dance. He needed to exude confidence, even if he had no idea what he was doing. The tango he could do. So, he remained confident in what he could control, no matter how little it turned out to be.

"I'm surprised you can dance," Sloane commented, her lips close enough to nibble at his ear.

He pressed closer to her, unsure if he wanted her or if he just didn't want her to escape. Or maybe it was a bit of both.

"Karen forced me to learn for our wedding," Andy said.

"I learned while spending time in Buenos Aires."

"That is as intimidating as it sounds." Andy commented, attempting to sound confident.

They gracefully moved about the empty wooden dance floor, the only people dancing. All eyes were on them. Hundreds of people gathered around to watch, unaware the dancers were no longer on the best of terms.

Andy ignored the stares. "I know what you have planned."

"Do you?" She asked, unconcerned.

"That's right. I'm not going to let you get away with it. These people aren't here for your game."

"Everyone is here for my game."

"This is serious."

"I don't care."

Andy's eyes widened and he leaned away from her crazed look. She was deranged and he had to find a way to stop her. Clearly she didn't care about anyone or anything. Only what she was after. He finally understood what he was up against, and it terrified him.

"These are people's lives," Andy said.

"And I'll play with them as I see fit," she said with a devious gleam. "And you're not going to stop me. There isn't any hope of anyone stopping me now."

"I will."

Sloane laughed.

The music reached its end and everyone turned to face the stage. Andy still held Sloane, his grip on her tighter.

"It's for your own good," Andy said.

"What do you know about doing anything for anyone?" Sloane asked.

Voices filtered out over the crowd from the stage, yet Andy didn't take his eyes off of Sloane.

"I'm attentive, caring. I provide for my family."

Sloane laughed again looking over his shoulder at the stage. "Wish Karen good luck for me."

Sloane spun away from Andy's grasp and walked off the dance floor.

A pop from the overhead speakers registered in Andy's eardrums shaking him from the trance Sloane had put him under. He looked up to the stage where Karen spoke to the crowd.

"And that's what I think I can do for this town," she said into the microphone, the reverb from the amplifier cancelling out her last words: "Thank you."

Both Karen and Jack were on stage for their debate. Karen had gone first. Andy had unknowingly been with Sloane during the entirety of Karen's opening statements.

"Shit," he swore to himself. "She's been talking the whole time?"

Andy looked around at the audience in attendance. There wasn't much of a reaction from the crowd. A few smatters of applause, but nothing more. Karen blushed. She looked down as she stepped away from the microphone. Jack stepped forward.

Andy moved over to the bar. Thomas Rosenbaum stood there looking smug, holding a glass of scotch on the rocks. He grinned ear-to-ear as Karen struggled.

"Looks like your girl is dying up there," Rosenbaum said, undoubtedly pleased to see a member of his household staff incapable of advancing in life.

Andy ignored him, shaking his head.

Jack moved to the microphone.

"My fellow citizens," Jack began, his voice powerful and regal. "I know times have been tough. I, myself, have felt the sting of this slow decline during the recession. I, myself, have postponed the expansion on my pool house. My pool house remains a mere four-thousand square feet.

"But we can get out of this. We can create lasting jobs to

sustain this once vibrant community. Think of it: Once upon a time, this town was bustling with A-list celebrities. Now we are relegated to only one A-lister, in I, myself. But we have a plan. Bring in the corporations which have done so well for so long—Wal-Mart, Ford Motor Company, Starbucks, CVS, Ikea, et cetera. Let them in, and let us prosper!"

The crowd erupted in applause. Jack took a bow and moved back.

Karen's eyes widened in shock as everyone cheered. They were completely satisfied with any strategy toward success.

"No, no, no," Karen said, moving to the microphone. "This is horrifying. I know we've all taken a loss in recent years, but I didn't really know it was this bad. You're all proud, hard-working business owners. And now you want to welcome in big businesses that will make you just another staff member?"

"Times are tough, what are we supposed to do?" A man in the middle of the crowd said.

"Tell 'em, Karen!" Susan shouted.

"I *will* tell you. We fix our roads. We fix our schools. We promote what this town was to the world. We remind the whole damn world what it used to mean to be proud of one's work."

Karen pointed at a man in the crowd. "Bob Foster, you owned the hardware store next to my father's shop. You owned that business for over thirty years. Everyone depended on your store for tools. But we all suffered, and we couldn't come to your store anymore. You went out of business. Now what do you do?"

"Lawn maintenance for the McDaniel's estate," Bob replied, sorrowfully.

"And Frances Gomez, you ran your own restaurant. You made some of the best pasta any of us will ever taste. But we all got hit by the recession, and no one could afford to eat something so delicious. What do you do now that you have gone out of business?"

"I make sandwiches for the Albertson's," Frances replied, with some embarrassment. "Sandwiches and nothing else."

"I could go on, but I think I've made my point. We're just working for a few, and not for everyone. We're no longer in business for the town, just a few wealthy families. We got hit, and we didn't know how to recover. Now, we've lost ourselves, our control, our dignity."

Some in the crowd began to nod and clap in affirmation. Andy had never seen Karen this fired up before and he swelled with surprise and pride. He beamed and wanted more from her, just as the crowd did.

"I say we show everyone in the whole damned world that the answer isn't to put on a name tag and become yet another replaceable staff member," Karen said, looking over to Thomas and Betsy, then to Andy.

As she locked eyes with him, Andy nodded for her to continue. He was tearing up, hanging on her every word. This was not the woman he knew. He only knew her as a nag, not an inspiration. Finally she'd become who she was always meant to be, and Andy got to witness it. He smiled and she smiled back. She would understand he supported her on this.

"We rise up. We stand proud of what we've accomplished because it will have been us who made this town great again, not some corporate stooge who's never lived here before. We do this. We control our own destinies. We leave something we made for our children. And if we fail, we pick ourselves up. We lift each other up, and we get back to work. Now tell me you wouldn't rather control your own lives!"

"Yeah!" the crowd answered.

"To leave something for your kids!"

"Yeah!"

"The workers, plumbers, electricians, the florists, and bakers. The ones who built this country, who don't need some rich yuppies to tell us how to ratchet a bolt or hammer in a nail."

"Yeah!"

"We do this. We work together. We build up this town ourselves!"

"Yeah!" The crowd erupted in cheers.

The hall grew deafeningly loud. There were still some who argued against Karen's ideas and the cheering morphed to yelling as those who disagreed became physical. The yelling became a roar, even louder than the storm outside.

Water flooded into the edges of the dining hall. Andy navigated through the pushing and shoving, frantically searching for Sloane. He knew if there was ever a time for her to do something nefarious, it would be when the whole town embattled itself. He moved through the crowd, determined to find her before she could do any more damage.

21

KAREN

Bedlam exploded in the dining hall as everyone turned from simply yelling their view points to tearing at each other. They moved like a torrential sea: A chaotic mass which could not and would not yield, not even to itself. Some argued against Karen's ideas and others argued for her. Those in favor were in the majority and cheered their praise. The cheering transformed into bellowing, while those who disagreed became physically violent.

Their combined noise of praise and rebuttal became a roar, even louder than the storm raging outside. Water flooded into the edges of the dining hall from under the floorboards. What started as light splashes became an inundation as it flowed inward, reaching every corner of the dining hall, exposing all in attendance to the wet elements.

Karen backed away from the microphone as the rowdy crowd rocked the stage. She stumbled farther from the front edge of the old wobbly stage and nearly lost her balance as Stanley shoved past her on his way to the microphone.

"All right, all right, everyone," Stanley boomed into the microphone.

The crowd did not cease. Everyone ignored the man on stage.

"Hey, damn it! That's enough already. The two sides have expressed their opinions. We'll all get a chance to have our voices heard on election day, whenever that will be." Stanley wasn't calming anyone down.

The fighting among those in the crowd continued.

"Okay, I've been nice so far, but this bullshit has gone on long enough. This was supposed to be a private fundraising function. For Jack. This was not supposed to be a gathering of all the most violent assholes in town. Now, if you'll all just shut the hell up already, we can move onto presenting the winner of the silent auction."

The pushing and shoving in the crowd turned into punching and kicking. Those who had known each other for years were now at each other's throats.

"Listen, you fucking assholes." Stanley turned red. "I'm talking here. You're all fighting because of the words of someone who wasn't even supposed to be here today. We will have the authorities brought here to arrest Karen Teague for inciting a riot. Is that what you idiots supporting her want?"

Karen continued stepping backward at Stanley's threats of detainment, not looking where she was going. After three feet, she unwittingly made it to the end of the stage. Her heel slipped and she struggled to find grip. Karen threw her arms up as her eyes widened and mouth opened to cry for help.

She violently fell off the three-foot stage, but was caught. Karen rested in the arms of another and was grateful for it. That was, until she discovered who caught her.

"Sloane?" She asked in shock.

"Yes, my darling?" Sloane returned, still cradling Karen in her arms with little effort.

Karen shimmed away from the woman's embrace and dusted herself off.

"I'm okay," Karen said, still disheveled.

"Are you, my darling?"

"I'm not your darling, damn it!"

"Touchy, touchy. I just came over to help."

"I would have been fine. It was just a few feet."

"Oh, not the fall to the ground. I was saving you from your fall from grace."

"What?"

"Yes, Karen, you've arrived only to be so easily smacked down. And I couldn't let that happen, could I?"

"So, you came to help me? How? Why?"

Karen looked at Sloane sideways. She'd been called a twat by Sloane earlier in the evening, and now she was being helped by the same woman who insulted her. Karen couldn't wrap her head around what Sloane's endgame could possibly be.

"Because we are sisters, you and I, that's why. As for how, I'll explain to you how easily you've been walked all over."

"It's Stanley's event." Karen was desperate. She had transformed the entire town into a crazed mob, instead of a group of inspired individuals. She invited any help she could get, even if it was from Sloane.

"Not just then on the stage." Sloane moved into Karen's space looking down her nose at the woman.

It unsettled Karen to be nearly chest to chest with Sloane.

"You've been walked on your entire life. By the rich, by the beautiful."

"Well, I'm kind of beautiful, right?" Karen said confidently.

"And even now you lie to yourself. This world has had its

way with you, and you've never even considered fighting back."

"What do you mean? I was. I was taking control of my destiny or whatever."

"You gave a cute speech, but you didn't go far enough. You could do and be so much more than a silly mayor, but only if you see the truth."

"What truth?" Karen was eager to learn some secret to Sloane's confidence.

"Fine, I'll tell you. It's a very personal story, and none of your business, but I'll tell you. When I was a younger woman, I was kidnapped by a group of rebels attempting to overthrow an African king in Africa. I was there, of course, as a peacekeeper, attempting to negotiate a trade agreement for the United Nations. I worked very closely with the king, as I was instructed to do. My negotiating skills were unmatched, and I knew exactly what to say and do to get what I needed.

"In short, I gave him the best love-making he'd ever had. The rebels must have gotten the wrong idea because they kidnapped me as an attempt at ransom, thinking he and I were a couple or something. Embarrassing, to think I would have been in a committed relationship with a king of such a small nation. I still get the giggles just remembering such a humiliating misunderstanding.

"The rebels had been fighting the king for over fifty years without a single victory, and this was their last best hope of gaining something after all those years. It really was quite pathetic. Anyway, I was held captive, something I'll never get used to. But I wasn't treated as an honored guest, as I thought I should have been. No, quite the opposite. I was enslaved. Bought and sold over and over again to whichever rebel had the fewest bullet holes in him that day. I gave them company. I washed their food and cooked their clothes. I did what I was told, and not once was I allowed to check my makeup in the mirror.

"The king waged a terrible war to retain me. You might have heard of the conflict, the Battle of the Three Rivers. No? It's in all the history books.

"Anyway, as the war waged on, I realized something. The rebel-leaders were only trying to get out of paying ridiculous sales taxes on high-end products by convincing others to die in battle for them. It was terrible what those rebel-leaders had to go through, and I could relate. So naturally, I assumed command of the rebellion. I brought them to victory over the king who loved me so dearly. So much so, he was even willing to make me his fifth wife out of six. A real upgrade. 'Better to be the fifth,' is what they always say.

"My point is, we took control over our destinies. I wasn't going to be dictated to, and neither should you. So, I want you to get up there on that stage. I want you to buck up and make them see that their lives can be better with you in charge. People need a sense of leadership – for someone to control them as they're led to freedom."

Karen frowned and nodded. She turned back to the stage to see the crowd of townspeople still roaring and unruly. Feeling dizzy and lightheaded, Karen stumbled backward. Sloane caught her again.

Karen wasn't sure she could even trust Sloane. She was dismissive and to a point, even cruel. She felt batted around like a pinball by Sloane, first being told this town needed to be uplifted, then later told, just not by her - that she was insignificant. Karen couldn't tell what Sloane's motives were, but the crowd was now rocking the stage to the point it was felt at the back. Someone needed to do something and it needed to be done quickly.

"You'll be fine. Just count down from ten. That always seems to get people to fucking focus," Sloane said.

Karen nodded again, stood up straight, and moved to the front of the stage. Halfway to the microphone, she turned back to Sloane.

Sloane nodded and waved her hand, urging her forward. "Take back your power, like I did."

Karen turned back around and gulped. She faced the crowd, staring them all down as she approached the microphone. Stanley was still trying to calm down the crowd, poorly. As she came up to his side, Karen placed her hand on his shoulder. He turned around suddenly, startled. She gave him a knowing look, and he yielded control of the microphone.

Stanley moved to the side with Jack. Karen looked at the crowd. No one paid any attention to her as she stood before them. Then she began as Sloane had suggested.

"Ten... nine... eight..."

Karen counted low and closely into the microphone. At first, she counted tentatively. But as she saw the small effect it had on some of the people in the crowd, she grew confident. Even so, the majority of people didn't pay any attention to her and still fought amongst themselves.

"Seven... six... five..."

She became impatient as she counted faster and louder. There was clearly frustration in the tone of her voice. More people in the crowd noticed this. More began to quiet down.

"Four... three... two..."

Many in the crowd now faced the stage, waiting anxiously for her to arrive at 'one.' Even Karen wasn't sure what would happen. She kept her demeanor commanding, standing up straight with a wrinkle in her brow and her tone of voice demanding attention. The crowd faced her, waiting. She wouldn't need to get to 'one.'

"Thank you for listening. I know we've all been through a lot, not just in the past few minutes, but maybe our entire lives. So, let me get to the point. For far too long we have been battling one another, ourselves. We each try to live up to an ideal set for us, whether it be by the last generation, or by society. Either way, this ideal is not set by each of us, as individuals.

"There have been a lot of ideas offered today – to go on with others, or to make a way for ourselves. To surrender again and again, or to stand tall and remember what we've done before.

"I know firsthand what it means to be beaten down by life. I left this town when I was eighteen, determined never to return, to make my life work on my own terms somewhere else. But I was back here living in my dad's house before my twenty-first birthday.

"When my father died, he was the last of the only family I had left. I took over his store, the only connection I had to this town and my dearly departed family. And after a few years, that was also gone.

"Then I found someone I thought I loved. He gave me my beautiful daughter. But after a few more years, my marriage ended, and my daughter wonders why her father doesn't live with us.

"I got a working job, doing something I'm over-qualified to do, and I get paid very little in exchange. I'm not complaining. No, I'm not going to complain. I'm not going to blame, or get angry, or get violent. I'm also not going to hide from my problems anymore."

Karen saw a figure move through the crowd. She held her breath for a moment, distracted by the sudden action. In a second, she recognized Andy as he hurriedly pushed his way through the dense throng. Her face lit up as he moved closer to the stage. She tried to lock eyes with him, but as he passed by to the backstage area, she realized he wasn't there for her. None of what she did was for him anyway, this was for her. She didn't need him, she never did. In that moment she felt like a fool for ever wasting her thoughts on him. She wouldn't make that mistake again, and returned her gaze back to the crowd.

"I'm not giving up anymore. I refuse to fail. I refuse to be told things can't be done a certain way, especially when I know in my heart and mind, I will succeed. That we will succeed. If any of you for a moment think we can't get done what I've suggested, let me remind you–"

The backstage doors slammed, reverberating in the hall.

"SLOANE!" a voice cried out.

Distracted, everyone in attendance looked past Karen. Jerry stepped forward to find out what was happening.

"I'll just see what that was all about," he said.

A muttering surged up from the crowd, but Karen was quick to retain their attention.

"Let me remind you we all have experience running businesses. We have the determination. We have each other to lean on. And we are already off to a great start. To begin with, tonight we're all here, in attendance, ready to forge a path to the future.

"We also have over three million dollars collected for this supposed fundraiser. I call to have that money allocated to public works. To finally rebuild this town to its former glory. To invest in this town's future by investing in this town's people.

"Let us not horde good fortune. But at the same time, no one gets a handout. No one has ever asked for one. We ask for a real representative democracy. All we ask is the opportunity. The opportunity to depend on hope over fear. Hard work over servitude. Unity over division.

"We are the same. We all live here. No more resentments toward one class of citizen from another class of citizen. No more vulgarities. No more calls for vengeance. No more raging against one another. We are one. We must work together. It's our time. It's our chance. It's our destiny. It's–"

"Our money!" Jerry exclaimed as he burst back into the dining hall, sweaty, out of breath, and doubled over clutching his knees. He breathed in deeply as he tried to regain his composure. All eyes focused on him as he straightened back up. "She took it. Sloane took the money and ran. Andy's chasing her."

The crowd turned back to Karen, who simply stared into space with a growing look of utter confusion.

"That bitch stole our money," Karen said to herself.

Karen didn't understand why someone who had given her so many words of encouragement would do something so devious. Thoughts raced in her mind at a thousand miles per hour, so fast she couldn't focus on any single one.

She replayed every interaction she'd had with Sloane, as few as there were. It was then Karen realized she had not only been lied to, but she had been led. Led directly to that moment on the stage. She wasn't meant to be a unifying voice, but a distracting one.

The look on her face grew into one of intense fury. Steam threatened to shoot from her nostrils and fire to burst from her mouth if given the chance. She clenched her fist to the point where her nails nearly broke the skin on her palms. Her knuckles blanched white, and her face steamed red. She clenched her jaw so tight she felt her teeth would grind to paste under the stress. Barely acknowledging the existence of the crowd, Karen realized this wasn't about what just happened to them, it was about what just happened to her. She had been played for a fool and used like a child's plaything. Many in the front row could likely see the capillaries in her crazed eyes about to burst as they glowed a bright crimson.

When Karen finally addressed the crowd, she would make everyone understand what had just happened. They, too, would feel the same sense of fury coursing through Karen's veins. Between the rich and the poor there was always a single unifier: Money. To take money from anyone slowly only made one resentful over time. To take it away all at once, and so much of it, would unify the townspeople into a rampage.

With all the rage she could muster, Karen offered a rally cry to incite the crowd.

"Get that bitch!"

22

ANDY

Andy made it to the backstage area as Karen spoke to the crowd. He understood exactly what Sloane was up to. Andy moved through the tight corridor and spotted her by Jerry's computer. She pulled a wire from a small black rectangular device and put it in her purse. Then she smashed the laptop to the ground, shattering the screen.

"SLOANE!" Andy cried. He sprinted after her. "Stop!"

Sloane turned to Andy. She glanced away from his gaze; a sign of brief hesitance. He looked at her with desperation; not able to let her go. To allow her to escape would be a betrayal by him to the people of Riders Bay. It would also be a betrayal to Sloane. In the space of a moment, he pleaded with her not to do this. Not to throw away whatever fondness they had left for each other. She looked back at him and smiled before hurrying out the back door, running into the rainy night. He'd lost her. She was gone; if he ever really had her in the first place.

The true scope of what Sloane just did hit Andy. He passed by the smashed laptop. She'd downloaded the financial information of all those who had donated that night. Now, she scurried off with all the money from the residents of Riders Bay. Rich, poor, it didn't matter. She robbed them all.

Andy chased Sloane out the back door, into the dark, rainy night. Even in the downpour, he could detect the faint hint of her perfume. It waned as she fled. He didn't want to let that glimmer of hope go. He didn't want her to go.

Sloane was his adventure; his beautiful nightmare that gave his heart reason to beat and made every pump of blood in his body worth the life it gave him. She could not be tamed, that much he knew. He didn't want to anyway. All he wanted was for her to be free, and he wanted to be free with her. But no matter how much freedom from his nearly useless life she provided, he still couldn't abide by her actions. It wasn't her money, and it was his responsibility to protect it.

Andy raced out in the pouring rain. The drops beat down on his head as he slipped on the pavement. Andy's labored breathing in the muggy air reminded him this wasn't his sort of thing; not chasing after anyone, not running at all. He ignored the usual shock of the cold running down his spine overridden by haste.

It didn't take him long to find Sloane dashing over to a taxi parked in the driveway of the Country Club. She yanked open the car door and forced the driver out of his vehicle. He resisted, pushing her back. Rain overwhelmed her hair and dragged down a blonde tendril. She swept it out of her sightline and, in an impatient rush, grabbed her handgun and squeezed the trigger. The man fell to the ground, clutching his wound, writhing.

Sloane scrambled into the car and peeled out of the slippery driveway. The taxi's backend fishtailed, bashing into a parked car. Pinwheels of water shot into the air from her rear tires as she made her escape from the Country Club.

Andy sprinted to his car slipping on the nearly flooded blacktop. He fumbled for his keys, awkwardly unlocking the door and slipping into the car. His wet hands barely grasped the steering wheel and shifter as he frenetically stabbed his keys at the ignition before he finally found pay dirt. Slamming on the gas, the engine limply coughed to life and he tore out of the parking lot after her.

Compared to Sloane's getaway ride, Andy's car had a lot to live up to. He'd have to push his vehicle to the redline to have any hope of catching up. Nonetheless, as Sloane charged down the short road leading out of the Country Club, Andy remained right behind her all the way. They made a sliding turn onto the road.

Andy's heart lodged in his throat, his stomach writhing like a scorpion's nest. This was beyond him. He'd never taken his car above the posted speed limit a day in his life. Not even the day he had to rush Karen to the hospital, the day Samantha was born – much to her annoyance. His very normal life was not going the way he thought it would. He asked his reflexes to do something of which they were incapable. Up until that moment, he controlled his own destiny. Now, his life belonged to Sloane as he gave chase. He prayed to whatever God would hear him to keep the car on the road, not expecting to be rewarded.

"Jesus," Andy exclaimed to himself breathlessly. "What the fuck am I doing?"

He knew this was probably Sloane's type of thing, but he screamed in his head, *Why the hell am I even doing any of this?* Letting her go would have been the safer option, but not honorable. Even if it killed him, which it quite possibly could, he would do everything in his power to catch her. And if a car wreck didn't do it, Sloane would most likely do it herself.

Andy focused on catching Sloane, no longer chasing her just to get the money back. It was far more personal. He couldn't let her go. Not after the damage she caused. Whether he could catch her or not, he knew his life was over anyway. No one would ever trust him with any amount of money again. He had provided a con woman access to the town's finances. This was no longer for the town or love, or whatever silly idea his father had put into his head; this was for his pride; this was for his own sense of justice. He wasn't like her. Andy wouldn't allow himself to take advantage of others. Therefore, he couldn't allow Sloane to either.

The road led to the empty and quiet Main Street, open for them to speed as fast as possible without any collateral damage. It was a blessing Andy took half a moment to acknowledge. The rain surged. The wipers were pointless. The wheel jerked with every pot hole hit, causing gushes of water to spray onto nearby parked cars. They hydroplaned, skirting the very edge of control. Luckily, Andy's tires pointed arrow-straight when they reconnected with the solid roadway.

The windshield fogged with his agitated, heavy breath. His eyes were pinned open as he silently begged the rain to let up just for a second – just so he could see where he was going.

Almost all other thought evaporated from his psyche. His brain turned to goo as blessings were counted that he wasn't already wrapped around an electrical post.

Sloane's car danced over the giant puddles with effortless grace. Andy could barely keep control of his gaze, never mind the steering wheel. His primal instinct to stay alive kept him that way. In the very back of his brain he clung onto his overall mission: *Don't let the far-more experienced Sloane get away.* He kidded himself thinking he wouldn't fail miserably.

In between bursts of light, Andy caught a glimpse of Sloane through his foggy windshield looking back at him. She laughed as her stolen car bucked with all horses in high-gear.

His once bottled disgust now boiled over. She mocked him. He was never really ever challenged to keep his word, but he would this day. Andy slammed his foot on the gas pedal, ramming hard into her vehicle. He would get that goddamned taxi to stop, one way or another.

Sloane's car swayed from side to side. Andy saw her shocked expression as she turned back to look at him. Then, with a grin and a nod, showed her esteem for the bold move. Something in Andy's heart ignited but he pushed it down. She regained control. He tried to hit her again and missed as she dodged the impact.

Losing ground, Andy pulled alongside her. His eyes flashed fury. He mouthed for her to pull over. She merely threw her head back and laughed again steering into him, smashing their cars.

Caught off guard, Andy momentarily lost control. Sloane made a hard right, leading off Main Street and down a back road that lead to the far end of town. As he regained control, he turned his car to follow. He knew exactly where she was headed.

23

KAREN

Karen led the townspeople of Riders Bay out of the Country Club to the parking lot. There she found people huddled over the bloodied taxi driver, still wailing in agony from the gunshot wound. An ambulance had been called, and it seemed to Karen, Sloane would stoop to any low to get what she wanted. Seeing this only focused her mounting rage.

"Stay with him until the ambulance gets here. Everyone else, to your cars. We're going to flip this town upside down to find Sloane if we have to. We'll get our money back and justice for him as well." Karen gestured to the taxi driver.

Storm-strength winds whipped her hair around. When she turned her head to avoid the pellets of rain and the smack of wind, her hair pinned to one side of her face. She alternated between moving her hair from her eyes and mouth to keeping her dress from flying up.

The pelleting torrent and the harshness of the wind

clattered like pots and pans. Karen's voice barely carried over the storm, and even she struggled to hear herself over the tempest gusts.

It wasn't her words, the sound of her voice, or even her tone that mobilized the townsfolk of Riders Bay. It was the glare in Karen's eyes. The way the storm clouds overhead seemed to darken further as she stomped through the parking lot inspired everyone to stumble to their cars. Karen's unadulterated rage made her one with the storm. She would not be halted, and her neighbors feared her glare falling upon them with her wrath quickly following if they did not get in line immediately.

They were going to catch Sloane, they were going to get their money, and they weren't going to let anyone walk all over them. Karen's piercing glare served as evidence she would ensure it.

"We're going to find that hell-bitch and bring her to justice. No one takes our hard-earned money and gets away with it!" she cried.

"Let's do this!" Debra returned.

"We're with you, Karen," Susan said. "Our car is over here at the end."

Thomas Rosenbaum moved over to Karen as others marched to their cars to search for Sloane.

"What is it, Thomas?" Karen asked before he could say anything. She reached Susan and Debra's car; they'd given her a ride to the Country Club.

"That was one hell of a speech back there. Very commanding. I always knew you had it in you," he commented, upholding what remained of his gruff exterior.

Karen wasn't buying it. She placed her hands on her hips and raised her chin as she waited, looking him dead in the eye. Something she wouldn't have dared do even an hour ago; but a lot had transpired since then. She certainly never had the chance to express her self-worth in years, feeling inadequate instead. Her demeanor changed and she exuded an expression which told Rosenbaum she wasn't a servant, and their employer-employee dynamic would no longer work for her. She demanded respect and would match his gruff demeanor with her own commanding stance.

"We're in a hurry," Karen said.

"Right, I was just wondering—" he began.

"If we could drive you home before we begin our search for the cunt who stole all our money? The answer is no."

"Of course not. I wouldn't ask you for something like that. This is a Ford Escort." Rosenbaum gestured at Susan and Debra's car. "I have a Bentley."

"Your vanity has been noted. Goodnight, Thomas." Karen opened the car door ready to slide in on the passenger side.

"I was wondering, if you'd let me ask, if you needed a ride from me?"

Karen frowned with an incredulous stare. This was an unexpected change in a man so rigid he could be made of stone. A very flabby stone, but stone nonetheless.

Thomas Rosenbaum softened. He alternated from placing his hands on his hips, to crossing his arms, then back, then pin straight to his sides, before finally settling on putting his hands behind his back.

As remarkable as Karen thought her change had been, somehow seeing him change into someone awkward and attentive was miraculous.

A matte blue Bentley Continental pulled up alongside Susan and Debra's old beater. Karen shook her head in astonishment. She wanted to snap a picture to remember this moment, but thought better of it, feeling it would be a tad cruel to rub it in and acknowledge how much he had changed. And her phone was out of power anyway. There was also the fear he'd revert to his old self if provided even the slightest degree of self-awareness.

Susan attempted to start the old car. The starter clicked,

and the motor whined, but the engine never turned over. The failing motor behind Karen mirrored the feeling that she failed to be independent. She rolled her eyes at Rosenbaum.

"Just accept the help," he said. "That's all I ever wanted to do. Help you. Help all three of you. Besides, we have some things to discuss."

Karen considered what it meant to accept any level of assistance from this man. She wondered if she took it would she be returning herself to the past dynamic of employer-employee? She didn't want that ever again.

As the old beater continued to sputter but not start, she also considered that Rosenbaum had more resources, and if she ever hoped to lead Riders Bay back to prosperity, she should take advantage of what she had in front of her, regardless of the source.

"What's the catch?" Karen asked.

"The catch is you let me deal with Sloane. I have a lot of powerful friends whom I would love to call in favors from. They'll tear her limb from limb. She won't live to breathe free air."

"Why am I handing her over to you? She stole from all of us."

"Yes, but the majority of the money she took was given by me. And I know just how to deal with people like her. Trust me, I've done it before." He glowered a look of self-determination. He was old, but he wasn't dead. "You don't get where I am without knowing how to bury your enemies."

"Figuratively or literally?"

He nodded and winked. "Exactly."

Karen suddenly felt twice as intimidated by him as usual. But for once they were on the same page. They both wanted blood.

"This car's not starting," Susan said, popping her head up from the driver's side.

"Maybe we can catch a ride from someone before everyone leaves?" Debra suggested.

Thomas lowered his brow and stared at Karen. "No matter what happens next, you'll have my vote."

"I thought you were all for gentrification," Karen replied.

"The only thing I'm for more than my own ideas are better ideas presented with conviction. You prove someone wrong by making them wrong."

"That's depressing."

"It also makes you rich. Now get in."

Karen gestured for Susan and Debra to follow Rosenbaum to his Bentley to go in search of their common enemy.

24

ANDY

The cars drove within inches of each other as they raced through the gate of the sparsely-used airfield.

The cracked tarmac covered in weeds, held almost faded lines just like the rest of the town.

Sloane led Andy along the edge of the airfield. She stayed away from the drainage ditch, skidding on the tarmac. Andy pulled back a little, moving away from the hazard as well. But as he looked down at the drainage ditch, he understood what he had to do. Andy accelerated and turned the wheel hard, aiming his car at her's once again. The nose smashed her rear corner panel.

Sloane's car fishtailed. She lost control, flipping over into the ditch. Mud and oil sprayed from the vehicle as it smashed into the dark sub-surface. The engine whined as it tumbled in the air and one of the tires ripped off its axel. Paneling from the old taxi tore off in the violent tumble. The front end of the cab caved in, inches away from the driver's side before it rolled onto its roof.

Andy stomped on the brake and flopped out of his car in a daze. He sprinted over to Sloane, panicking; his heart still in his throat and his head dizzy with terror. *What have I done? Did I kill her?* He looked down at the mangled destruction of the taxi, and quickly did the mental math to determine if a crash of this severity was one someone could survive.

The rain eased, and the clouds began to part. For the first time in days, the sky cleared, and stars shone over Riders Bay. As the rain finally stopped, sheens of sweat coated Andy, replacing the rain water with the sheer horror of what he'd just done. The sky flashed with cascading stars. It was peaceful, but Andy couldn't take even a moment to appreciate it. He needed to know if Sloane was dead or alive.

Then he heard the satisfying sound of life.

"Bloody mother fucker!" Sloane cried from inside the overturned taxi.

There was a rumble from the car doors before Sloane finally pulled herself out through the window of the overturned taxi. She crawled away from the car, clutching her purse. Mud marred her ripped, short dress as she struggled to claw out of the ditch. Blood coated her upper brow. Mud now replaced her makeup, and her once professionally styled hair clung to her head. She looked like a beast emerging from a cave after hibernation. She sounded like one as well.

"What the fuck! Are you fucking kidding me!"

She hobbled up out of the muddy ditch, slipping a few times before finally kicking off her heels. Ultimately she gained traction by digging her once beautifully manicured toes into the sides of the slick ditch.

"I was going to ask you the same thing," Andy said breathlessly. He scrambled over to her as she finally escaped the drainage ditch. "I'm sorry, but I had to stop you."

"Well, you succeeded." Sloane's ire laced her words, harsh

and husky. Her eyes narrowed with piercing fury. Laboring to breathe, she touched her head to check for blood. She swatted Andy's hand away as he dabbed her forehead with his tie. He kept trying until finally she relented. Her furious scowl softened, and Andy returned the look with his own sorrowful compassion. Then she stalked past him, the moment gone and her mind back on the job.

Sloane moved past Andy to his car. She rummaged through her purse on the trunk before pulling out a cigarette case and a lighter. She looked through her purse more exuberantly before sighing with relief. She found what she was looking for.

"Yes," Sloane exclaimed as she gazed up to the clear night's sky. "It's all been worth it." She pulled out a cigarette and handed the lighter to Andy. At first, he didn't know what to do with it, until she put the cigarette in her mouth and leaned forward slightly. She waited for him to be a gentleman, or something more demeaning than a gentleman. He flicked on the lighter, lit her cigarette, and flicked it closed. Sloane took a deep puff holding it in for a long while before exhaling through her nostrils. She tilted her head back and closed her eyes. Relief combined with an air of annoyance clung to her every pore. Andy just hoped this was almost over.

"What's all this really about, Sloane?" He asked after a beat.

"You're sweet, but you're a complete moron," she said, stroking her brow.

A large black SUV pulled up next to Andy's poor excuse for a car.

"Who the bloody hell is this?" Sloane asked, annoyed.

The doors opened and Jackson, Juan, and Carl hopped out. Andy stood up straight. He nervously watched them, not sure whether to stay put, run, or fight, finally deciding instead to follow Sloane's lead.

"Ah, fuck. Boys, I'm really not in the mood right now," Sloane said as she threw her head back in frustration.

"Should we do something?" Andy asked nervously.

Andy stood closer to Sloane as he looked deep into her emerald gaze. He hoped she'd have an idea to get them out of trouble. They felt one another's heat radiate as the space between their bodies grew smaller. Andy didn't think for a moment she understood how he felt about her. That even though he hit her into a ditch, he did care about her.

"I'll take care of this. Hold my purse." Sloane shoved her carryall against his chest.

Andy fumbled with it for a while before finally getting a hold of the inexplicably heavy bag. Sloane walked toward Jackson on the balls of her feet, an attempt to replicate wearing high heels or an unconscious reflex. Her hair suctioned to her face was brown with mud, the shoulder of her dress hung torn, and what was left of the top of her sheath barely clung to her chest. Yet Sloane held her chin high and moved gracefully with an air of superiority. She remained in command.

"Where is it, Sloane?" Jackson asked. "Where's my money?"

"You know what, Jackson?" Sloane said as she marched up to the man. "I've had it up to here with you and your bullshit!"

Sloane's graceful, tip-toed footsteps hastened in her anger. Her chin lowered as she glowered at her target. Jackson relaxed his posture, and that only made her more aggressive. She raised her hands slowly and methodically. She might have wanted to rip his head off, but settled for a more practical and less messy action. Sloane pushed him hard in the chest, nearly losing her cigarette in the process.

"It's not my fucking fault you were all too fucking stupid to use the equipment you asked for," Sloane screamed into Jackson's face.

Juan and Carl looked on in shock. Jackson simply avoided eye contact with Sloane in shame. Sloane would now go in for the kill.

"No. Fucking. Refunds," she said, and with each word she again shoved him in the chest.

Another car pulled up next to Andy's. The doors opened, and out stepped Special Agents Thompson and Russell.

Sloane threw her hands up in the air. She rolled her eyes and threw back her head.

"Well, of course. This keeps on getting better and better. Come on, boys. Join the party."

"Sloane," Special Agent Thompson said as he and Special Agent Russell moved over beside her. "It is with great pleasure that I tell you you're under arrest. You have the right to remain silent–"

"Yes, yes, yes. Blah, blah, blah."

"Don't do that! Don't interrupt me. I've been waiting too long for this," Special Agent Thompson snapped.

"Calm down." Special Agent Russell put a hand on Thompson's shoulder.

"No, I'm not going to calm down," Special Agent Thompson cried, shaking away Russell's hand on his shoulder. "She's disrespecting us."

"Yeah, Thompson, relax. You got me," Sloane said. She turned to Andy and gave him a look. Her tone, her eyes, they all said something. A moment passed before he realized what the look meant. It was a sentiment he wasn't ready to accept.

It was goodbye.

Special Agent Thompson put handcuffs on Sloane's wrists.

The slap of the metal sounded louder for some reason, more like the slamming of a steel trap or a jail cell. It was the sound of finality. It was ending, or that maybe it was already over. Andy nearly collapsed, unable to prevent anything bad from happening to anyone. His failure crushed him like an ACME anvil.

"I've been waiting five years for this moment," Special Agent Thompson said.

"Only five? I thought you'd been after me for over ten?" Sloane returned.

"What?"

"Morocco. That ring any bells?"

"Goddammit! We've been hunting you down for over twelve years?"

Sloane threw her head back in manic laughter.

Special Agent Thompson pulled out his phone, dialed a number, and talked to someone on the other end.

"You can come out now," Special Agent Thompson said. "We're ready to go."

A G5 jet taxied out of a nearby hangar.

"There's our ride. We're taking you directly to the field office. Get her purse, Russell."

Special Agent Russell snatched her purse from Andy's grasp, and marched over to the now-parked jet.

Jackson and his men backed away from the situation as they walked to their car, unwilling to deal with the Feds. Once they were in their SUV, they sped off, fleeing the airfield.

Andy stood on the tarmac alone for the first time in what felt like an eternity. His eyes filled with tears and his breathing drew shallow. He doubled over trying to get a grip and come to terms with what was happening. Then he looked one more time as Sloane was escorted away. He couldn't let her go, not so soon.

He stood up straight and found life again in his lungs. Blood circulated to his legs, and to his balls. He wasn't going to let her go like this, having fought too hard to let it end so suddenly.

"Wait!" Andy yelled.

He ran to Sloane as she turned around. He embraced her strong and passionately kissed her. This was, for all he knew, the last time they'd ever share such a kiss. Every fiber of his being pressed against her body. He wanted to share his warmth with her one last time, he wanted to hold her, to embrace their last moments. To his surprise and delight, she returned the passion, lifting her cuffed hands over his head, pressing her body harder against his. He wasn't quite sure, but perhaps she didn't want to let him go either.

"I don't understand," Andy whispered beside her cheek. "I thought you said these guys weren't really FBI."

"I lied, Andrew. I lied about a lot of things. Hell, I lied about everything," Sloane said.

"Why? Why lie?" Andy asked pulling back.

"To get you to help me. A lot of good that did."

"And you never really wanted me?"

"You never really wanted me either."

Andy sensed the anger under her tone. He needed to quell that fire, not wanting their final moments to end in mistrust.

"That's a lie," Andy confessed.

"Excuse me?" Sloane asked taken aback.

"I lied about wanting to get back with Karen. Lied to myself. I was afraid to get close to you."

Sloane's eyes welled up.

"When I do what I do, people usually want to stay away from me, or arrest me, or execute me," Sloane said.

"Not me." Andy tenderly put his hands on either side of her face. "I want you. We'll figure this out."

"Well, I'm being arrested."

"We'll figure that out, too."

"Andrew, you really are the sweetest man I think I've ever met. I truly mean that. But you are also the dumbest. Everything I do every day is for money. I can't ever stay in the same place for more than a week because there's always someone after me. Then there's people like you, whom I use, and I can't get close to because it isn't in my nature. There isn't a single thing I've told you that's true. I hurt you, I know that. I hurt everyone. I wish I could be sorry, but it would take something I do not possess to be able to apologize."

"All right, let's go. I have a lot of paperwork I need to bury you under," Thompson said, pulling Sloane's arms up over Andy's head and dragging her away toward the private jet.

As she was torn from Andy, she simply shrugged in the absence of his arms. That was the way she would leave his embrace, with a shrug.

The clear sky reflected a wet runway. The air cooled and everything seemed wrapped in a blue hue. Warm breaths alighted from everyone, and Andy shivered a little. He placed his hands in his pockets to keep them warm.

A part of him wanted this horrible moment to last forever. To see her as she was, not how he might see her later on, in a prison jumpsuit. Though he was sure she'd look fantastic in bright orange. She always looked fantastic.

They were halfway up the staircase to the jet when Andy stumbled forward. "Sloane!" He called after her, torn apart by the very idea that once she was gone it would be for good, and so were his chances at ever having anything but a normal life. No more adventure, and certainly no more life with Sloane leaving him for good.

With every fiber in his being Andy cried out, "I think I love you!"

"My darling," Sloane said as she looked over her shoulder at him. She flashed him one last sultry look before she boarded the jet. "You only think you love me?"

25

KAREN

From sedan to big-rig truck, the once-empty streets of Riders Bay teemed with life as nearly every vehicle prowled through the darkened Main Street. Every driver of every car, and every passenger of vehicles filled beyond capacity peered from their dirty windows in search of any trace of the woman.

The woman who'd stolen their hard-earned money.

The woman who'd set them all up to fail.

Thomas' driver took the Bentley down Main at half-speed. Cars followed closely behind with people shouting from their windows which areas of the town they'd cleared in the short time they searched.

"Where could this bitch be?" Karen asked.

She sat comfortably between Susan and Debra. The spacious backseat provided more room than any of them ever experienced in a car. Rosenbaum rode in the front with the driver; he hadn't sat in the front seat of a car since he was in his early thirties. He leaned unusually close to the dashboard, amazed at the perspective.

"These roads really are bad. You can get a better sense of it from all the way up here," he said.

Rosenbaum glanced at his driver, catching the end of an eye roll. He merely shook his head and pursed his lips, gazing back on the terrible roads of Riders Bay.

Karen balled a fist and hit her open hand. "We have to find this bitch. She's got to be somewhere around here, that bitch. Has anyone checked if that bitch is still at the hotel?"

"Could you ease up on the bitch stuff? We get it, you hate her. Swearing doesn't suit you," Debra said.

"I don't think I've ever heard you cuss before," Susan chimed in.

"Yeah, sorry. I'm not very good at it. I think the last time I called someone a bitch was in junior high. And even then, I mumbled it."

Debra and Susan were on their smartphones texting anyone with whom they could get in contact.

"Mary checked the hotel," Debra said, reading a text. "It's been trashed but she's not there."

"Mary?" Susan asked, suspiciously.

Debra looked away shamefully.

"Told you Susan would be jealous," Karen said.

"We'll talk about that later," Susan said, expressing a tinge of resentment, but forgiving all the same.

With some effort due to the comfort of the seat, Karen leaned toward the front of the town car.

"Do you have any ideas?" Karen asked Rosenbaum, who turned to his driver, who merely shrugged.

"It's a small town. There aren't many places to go. I have some friends blocking every exit. She can't drive out," he said.

"And she won't hike through the forest," Karen said.

"How do you know?"

"Because I've met her. Trust me. She's never walked farther than from her seat to the liquor cart. What about the ferry?"

"We've got people there, too."

"Then she's hiding. We'll just have to wait her out."

She now knew what kind of woman Sloane was: A coward. Karen anxiously seesawed back and forth from her seat to the front of the car. She wanted Sloane, but also to show the people of Riders Bay they would get their justice. Karen wanted the justice for herself, but needed to find her enemy first.

"There is one other way she could get out of town," Rosenbaum said reflectively.

"What is it?" Karen asked.

"The airfield."

"I completely forgot about that."

"Don't blame yourself. You don't own a plane. I do."

"You were doing so well."

"Sorry."

Karen leaned back, now allowing herself a moment to truly relax in the luxurious comfort.

"Let everyone know Sloane's at the airfield. We're headed there now," Karen relayed to Debra and Susan.

They both furiously texted the message. Rosenbaum gestured for the driver to hurry along to the private airfield on the other side of town.

KAREN BEAMED with anticipation as the assembly of cars sped through the darkened, narrow road leading to the entrance of the tarmac. Rosenbaum's Bentley led the way, and dozens of cars followed. Once through the narrow front entrance, the vehicles split off, their headlights flooding the runway with yellow light.

The Bentley stopped as the driver noticed a figure standing in the middle of the runway. The other cars followed suit. A man stood with his back to them, hands in his pockets. He stared forward as a small jet picked up speed and took off into the air. His gaze followed it into the star-filled sky. As it left view, his head bowed, and his posture slumped before he turned to everyone gathered behind him.

Karen recognized the slumped silhouette instantly. She looked at Andy as he stood in the middle of the tarmac, wondering if he'd lost something more than just money that night. Then her feelings of sentimentality fled, and an immediate sense of pragmatism entered her veins like a transfusion. She didn't give a damn about his stupid love life. There was a duty here to preform to ensure everything was going to be all right. By the look of his sullen demeanor, it didn't appear to be good news.

Andy turned toward the assembly of parked cars.

"What the hell are you all doing here?" Andy asked, surprised at the sight of so many people.

Karen and the others hopped out of the Bentley.

"We were about to ask you the same thing. Where's Sloane? Was she on that plane?"

"Yeah."

"And you just let her get away?" Karen asked, fury engulfing her more and more.

She turned her newfound livid glare upon Andy, but he didn't seem to respond to it. Then she thought perhaps the glare was something she discovered while married to Andy, and therefore he was immune. She didn't care. She prowled over to him slowly, not entirely sure what she would do when she got to him.

"I didn't let anything happen," Andy snapped back.

"She took all of our money," Karen said, still slowly moving toward him.

"Yeah."

"Yeah? That's all you have to say? Yeah?"

"She was arrested. Taken by those FBI guys. Everything will be all right. Eventually."

"Hey, dumb-shit!" Karen screamed.

"Excuse me?"

"Where's the hard drive?"

"Huh?"

"Jerry said she took our financial info. Downloaded it to a portable hard drive. Did the Feds take that, too?"

"They didn't mention it."

"Did you?"

"Uh–"

"What the fuck!"

Andy turned back to the sky, then back to Karen. She could see the wheels turning in his mind as he arrived at the conclusion she'd reached minutes earlier. Karen could tell he now realized the scope of his mistake as his eyes widened in disbelief. He hadn't done his job, and he had been a completely useless moron to Karen, once again.

Sloane had one fool left to trick, and she'd done so masterfully.

"Uh…" Andy's voice trailed off, unable to find reassuring words to rectify his blunder.

Karen marched over to Andy, placed her hands around his throat, and throttled him. She pushed him to the ground, punching and kicking him as he writhed. The townspeople behind them merely looked on from their cars, their headlights bathing the beating an ex-wife gave her ex-husband for his stupidity.

26

SLOANE

Sloane looked out the window as the jet headed toward the runway. She saw the dopey yet lovely look of heartwarming desperation on Andy's face, then closed the shade on the window, the cuffs on her wrists clinking.

She didn't want to see him again.

Sloane sat in the immaculate jet, lounging in the plush, white leather seating with enough space for each of the three passengers to stretch out and rest on the long flight. Her seat was dirty from the mud covering her from head to toe. The high-pressure air conditioning in the cabin dried it into a hard shell.

She hated being dirty.

Sloane also hated being handcuffed. She lifted her limbs toward Thompson.

"Un-cuff me already."

Thompson took out the key from his pocket, reached over,

and unlocked the cuffs. He placed them on the empty seat next to him.

"You got my purse, right, Russell?" She asked.

"Yes, Sloane," Russell said, his tone and demeanor less uptight than before. "You know I wouldn't forget it."

"And the hard drive?"

Russell rummaged through her purse before pulling out the portable drive.

"Right here," Russell answered.

Sloane clapped and smiled gleefully.

"Take very good care of that. You wouldn't imagine what I had to do for it."

Russell reached for a briefcase next to him, opened it, and placed the hard drive inside for safe keeping.

"As soon as we land, we need to hurry with the accounts before the banks close them." Sloane told him.

"I'll take care of it," Russell replied.

Sloane leaned back in her seat and reclined it. She put her feet up onto Thompson's lap. As she took stock of what she'd accomplished over the weekend, he massaged her feet – knocking off bits of mud as he did.

"Before you get too comfortable, do you want to tell me where we're supposed to be going, Señorita Sloane?" A voice said from the cockpit.

The pilot turned from his seat. The jet reached the runway, now ready for take-off.

"We need to go down south, Enrique," Sloane told the pilot. "To Montoon. We have to leave the country for a while to count all the money."

"Yes, Señorita Sloane," Enrique said, smiling, very much alive and well.

"I'm sorry about last night. I hope it didn't hurt too much when I shot you."

"I'm still a little sore. You could have chosen a fattier place to shoot me."

"I had to make it look real. You should count yourself lucky I even managed to change the ammunition to the rubber bullets. I had to do all that shuffling in my purse."

Enrique flashed his handsome smile and turned back to the controls.

The engines whined as the plane raced down the runway. In a matter of moments, it lifted off and soared into the sky. It banked as it headed south.

Sloane lifted up the shade to look down on all she wrought.

She could see the now-empty town. Broken, left in despair and disrepair. From the sky, it seemed as though it might have been quaint once upon a time. She watched the gathering of cars on the tarmac below; supposedly the townspeople's last attempt to capture her. At first, she gasped, taken aback by the assembly mobilized on the runway, obviously with the expressed purpose and expectation of capturing her. After a short moment of reflection, Sloane shrugged indifferently and pulled the shade back down. Their problems weren't her problems.

"Another job well done," Thompson said.

Sloane didn't respond.

"Sloane?"

"Yes, Thompson. Another good job, team. We did what we came here to do. And now we move on," she said, more to herself than to anyone else.

"What the hell was with Jackson?" Thompson asked.

"He said we gave him faulty equipment," Sloane answered, focused more on cleaning the dried mud out from under her fingernails than on Thompson.

"What? No way. That was the good stuff."

"Thompson, Thompson, Thompson. You still have so much to learn. Of course, I gave them the faulty equipment."

"What?"

"That stuff wasn't going to work. I was lucky I could even

get the demo to function. One of his guys even exploded or whatever."

"Idiots," Thompson remarked.

Sloane, Thompson, and Russell laughed.

"Luckily, Jackson doesn't know what any of my boys look like." Sloane gestured to Thompson, Russell, and Enrique. "Otherwise we would have had a bloody shoot out."

They laughed at the idea of mortal danger.

"Fools," Thompson commented. "Probably can't use that trick twice."

"Oh, dear, do you really think I do anything more than once?"

They laughed some more.

"Those morons," Thompson said.

Sloane really did think they were lucky, an occurrence she never wanted to depend on. Jackson had been a pain in her ass and she didn't mind screwing him over one last time. She'd be unable to use the same trick again, as Thompson had eluded. But she had no intention of playing any trick, any con, more than once. She was far too creative for that. Never the same lie twice.

And on the other hand, she had zero inclination of ever crossing paths with the criminal likes of Jackson for any reason, at any time, whatsoever. Sloane had a mild level of professional respect for him, but it didn't go any further than that.

"Well, you sure did pick the perfect mark for this last job," Thompson said.

"Yes, I suppose I did," Sloane said, casually, hiding a sudden quiver of her lip.

She meant to be flippant, but internally a war raged. Clinging onto a nature she'd been building for years. In a single weekend she'd somehow forced herself to examine who and what she was meant to be. The walls within her were crashing down, and she struggled to hold onto her composure.

On the tarmac below stood a man who wanted her, despite being utterly flawed. He was nothing like her. They were from two different worlds; worlds as far apart as they could get. Yet, she wanted to be someone she wasn't, just for him, even if that wasn't something he would ever ask from her. He just wanted her, and she fought against the volcanic sensation that she wanted him as well.

"It was an inspired idea for you to get us to pressure the accountant," Thompson commented.

"I needed to force his hand." Sloane held in all emotion as she explained. "Confusing him into believing that authority figures couldn't be trusted was the only way to ensure his loyalty. And, of course, he would do as I told him, even if he was beginning to wise up to my scheme."

"I mean, what a moron. Was he that stupid or are you that good?"

Sloane simply raised an eyebrow at Thompson.

"Right, you're that good," Thompson said in understanding. "But he fell in love with you. He only knew you for a few days."

"It only takes a few minutes. You should know that better than most."

Sloane only half meant it, retreating back behind her armor. Then she relaxed, lowering her shoulders, relieving the tension in her face, and taking a deep breath. She fiddled with the shade for a few seconds lost in all thought except to flirt with the prospect of checking on who was still down below. She finally did draw open the shade and looked out the window.

The sky cleared over Riders Bay for the first time in days. All to show what the place had become. The once broken town had found itself in its haste to capture its greatest villain. The lights were on again; lights that came from the people. Though the lights acted as torches in search of Sloane, it was enough to provide the small town with hope for the future. They were united in one cause: Sloane, and her immediate arrest. But it was never going to happen.

She felt no guilt. Not for a single moment. But as the jet leveled off in the clouds, Sloane looked out of the window and felt something she couldn't remember ever feeling before. A sensation of longing and loss. She'd gained something more than all the money in the town; she gained a fondness for a sweet and unassuming man. Perhaps deep down inside of her, it was more than that.

Sloane had a connection with Andy. He'd trusted her, and like the fool she thought he'd be, he'd abided by her every whim. It was as it always was; so why did it feel different this time? She hated being cemented in self-doubt more than she hated being covered in mud. Putting Andy out of her mind, she wanted to let the thought of him go. But as she felt the plane rise higher into the air, thoughts of him only followed. It wouldn't matter how far she traveled from him, Andy would always be on her mind and in her heart.

"I hope we get another mark half as dopey as that Andy guy," Thompson said.

"No one gets that lucky," Sloane said.

"You always say luck's got nothing to do with it."

"I say a lot of things."

"Well, you sure know how to pick them," Thompson said. "I actually think he was in love with you. I know you're hot and all, but how did you get him to fall that hard?"

"The secret is you have to meet them halfway. Sometimes a little more than halfway, if the situation calls for it."

As she saw the last tiny glimpse of Andy a mile away, Sloane realized he hadn't been the only fool. The utter anguish of heartbreak swelled within her; she found it impossible to quell her eruption of emotion. Regret hit her hard as she pulled down the shade to the window one last time, never to look on Andy or the quaint town of Riders Bay again. She'd never see him again, and that thought struck her like a meteor. The costly error of feeling something for her mark had been made. Sloane felt like an idiot, as she muttered to herself.

"Shit."

ABOUT THE AUTHOR

Nicholas Kurch is a writer of various genres, both fiction and non-fiction. He has written for publications such as ClutchPoints and The Manifold Magazine.

He is currently working on the follow-up to his debut book, SLOANE, launching 2019. Raised in Hawaii, he attended the University of Hawaii-West Oahu.

Nick, as he likes to be called, is a boring man, with not much going on. He lives vicariously through his ridiculous characters and their misadventures. If you wanted to, though he couldn't see why, you can follow him on Twitter @KurchNick.

https://nickkurch.weebly.com

https://twitter.com/KurchNick